Music Lesson

A list of books in the series appears at the end of this volume.

MUSIC LESSON

Stories by
Martha Lacy Hall

UNIVERSITY OF ILLINOIS PRESS
Urbana and Chicago

C . 2

*Publication of this work was supported in part
by grants from the National Endowment for the Arts
and the Illinois Arts Council, a state agency.*

This book is printed on acid-free paper.

"Privacy," *Sewanee Review* 93, no. 1 (1983).
"Music Lesson," *New Orleans Review* 7, no. 1 (1980).
"The Painter," *Southern Review* 15, no. 2 (1979).
"Joanna," *Southern Review* 19, no. 3 (1983).
"The Peaceful Eye," *Southern Review* 6, no. 4 (1970).
"The Man Who Gave Brother Double Pneumonia," *Southern Review* 19,
no. 2 (1983).

Library of Congress Cataloging in Publication Data

Hall, Martha Lacy, 1923–
Music lesson.

(Illinois short fiction)
Contents: Privacy—Music lesson—The painter—[etc.]
I. Title. II. Series.
PS 3558.A3716M8   1984   813'.54   83-24151
ISBN 0-252-01129-5

For Bob

Contents

Privacy

Before I can press open my paperback I hear Miss Ada Maude's Continental throb quietly into Miss Coralie's driveway, then sigh into silence, its baby-blue gloss barely visible through the dense foliage of the Pride of Mobiles that separate us.

I settle back to read in my lawn chair, amid fig trees and shrubbery, the ripe-banana odor of fuscatas blending with the gentle spice of sweet olives in Miss Coralie's yard next door. The summer afternoon is made cooler by the sweep of the old Emerson oscillator that I have stationed on a fairly level pecan stump, relic of a historic windstorm. An extension cord drapes over a camellia from an outlet in the toolshed.

I watch the thick St. Augustine turf darken in the four o'clock shadow of Mr. Henry George Kell's house, which rises three gingerbread stories tall at my back — Mr. Henry George, who fought alongside my father in the Battle of the Bulge, who wears an eyepatch over his wound, an empty eye socket or ruined eyeball, and who likes to play Handel's music in the early evenings, the Water Music flowing out the bay window of his library and over the ivied wall that gives us both privacy.

I know that Miss Coralie is in her swing on her side porch, because I can hear the gravelly whine of the chain as she gives herself the slightest push now and again. I am thinking, as I often do, that we have a special neighborhood, only three houses on a whole square, I on a corner, Mr. Henry George at my back, Miss Coralie and Mr. Buddy beside me, and the rest a playground, rather triangular, for children we never see and seldom hear. I was born here and have lived her for forty years, the last six alone, but not the least bit lonely. I read and I write; I am interested in the town, and I often have lunch or tea with Miss Coralie. I go to Mr. Henry George's at Christmastime.

As I hear the car doors open and shut I am thinking that someone who didn't know would never guess that Miss Ada Maude and Miss Coralie are sisters. Miss Coralie is quiet, dark, slender, quick of movement, rather ageless, though I know she was eighteen when I was born. Miss Ada Maude is clabber white and heavy, and certainly not quiet. Since her arthritis has gotten bad she has had a driver, Walter, and when she comes to see Miss Coralie he sits in the car, or she tells him he can walk downtown for thirty minutes and get a Coke out of the machine at the Gulf station. I have been caught at Miss Coralie's more than once when Miss Ada Maude comes for her Monday afternoons.

As Miss Ada Maude's foot comes down heavily, hollowly, on the first wood step, I am hearing her begin, in her choir contralto, on Mr. Buddy.

"Coralie, when are you going to get these porch steps painted? Buddy would let this place rot and fall down. Doesn't he ever do anything on this whole earth but drink beer at Bugga's and play cards every single night including Sundays down at the line? It's just as well Papa was spared seeing you living like this . . ."

I can barely hear Miss Coralie: "Afternoon, Sister. Pleasant weather for late June, isn't it? Just look at the crape myrtles." Miss Ada Maude is on the porch. "Take a rocker. I've just washed and ironed the covers."

I hear the wicker protest under Miss Ada Maude's weight, and I hear her heels come down on the porch floor, beginning a rhythm that will punctuate her afternoon's exhortations. I don't have to actually see these two to know how they look, seated amid nodding fronds of Boston and fishtail ferns, a background of gray clapboard wall, Miss Ada Maude in a flowered sheer, her blue hair in a tight perm, her white powder splotched with two rouge spots, 12-millimeter faux pearl earbobs, three or four nondescript platinum filigree rings that match the little watch belted around her plump freckled wrist. Miss Coralie is probably wearing Keds, slacks, and a plaid shirt. She is very likely to be mending one of the white oxford-cloth shirts that Mr. Buddy wears to town everyday, or maybe working a neat monogram on the pocket.

"Now Coralie, I'm older than you are, and I've got eyes to see and ears to hear, which you seem to lack. There's something I am going to have to tell you. I had firmly made up my mind not to, but I decided it would be better for you to hear it from me than from someone else." Miss Ada Maude pauses, clears her throat. Miss Coralie says nothing, and I can see her gently arched eyebrows lift slightly. I am thinking that I should leave. I settle back.

"Buddy pulled a stunt yesterday that has everybody in town talking. He is a laughingstock. And of course when this town laughs at him, it is laughing at you. And at me."

"Ada Maude . . . ?"

"He relieved himself against the post office wall — right after noon when most of this town's respectable people were going home from church, including myself — your sister, the daughter, granddaughter, and widow of three of this town's most revered citizens. I had Olga and Neva Chichester in my car with me, taking them home from church, two absolutely perfect and patrician ladies — you cannot deny that — who don't even permit a TV set in their house, and just as we pulled up at the post office for Walter to pick up their mail for them, what do we behold but my sister's husband turned around to this dark wet spot on the brick wall between the first two pittisporums, just, just . . ."

"Urinating," says Miss Coralie. And I am hoping she will tell me about this conversation later, in her own words, knowing she can never dream I have sat here eavesdropping, needing to leave, not wanting to leave, and knowing that if I do she and Miss Ada Maude might hear me, and Miss Ada Maude, who has not cared for me ever, but particularly not since I divorced her late husband's nephew six years ago, will find the most cutting way possible to let me know what she thinks of people lurking about in the shrubbery, listening.

"Drunk. At noon on Sunday. Either that or he's gone completely out of his mind."

Miss Coralie says, "Oh my, Ada Maude. And the Chichesters with you."

"*Oh my? Oh my?* Is that all you have to say? What is the matter with you, Coralie?" Miss Ada Maude has stopped rocking. I can see her light blue eyes bugging out behind her thick lenses. "Don't you realize we are humiliated? For thirty-five years you've sat here and let that . . . that reprobate spend practically every nickel Papa left you. He hasn't worked a lick at a stick since poor Papa's coffin was lowered into his grave. Just dolls himself up like a dandy twice a day and heads for Bugga's, hangs around that trashy café with the riffraff of this town till somebody gives him a ride down to Goat's at night to play . . . play . . ."

"Bourée."

"Well, whatever. And you are content to just sit here like a common person, wearing pants and working in your front yard like a field hand. No help in your house; never darkening the church door; a woman by herself in this house till all hours every night. Sometimes I . . ." Miss Ada Maude runs out of wind and can't finish.

Miss Coralie is saying, "Now Sister, you exaggerate. I am not unhappy. I take my little trips in the spring and the fall . . ."

"But always alone!" Miss Ada Maude is rocking again.

"I like working in my yard. You know that, Sister. I don't need a maid. And you know I like my privacy. Didn't you tell me you were bringing me a recipe?"

"What? Oh, yes." And I can hear her unsnapping her big handbag.

"Purple-hull pea hull jelly."

"Purple-hull pea hull jelly?"

"Yes. Just a minute. I've got it here somewhere. It sounds wonderful. After you shell your peas, you boil the hulls till they are mush. Then you strain the mush through cheesecloth. That gives you your stock."

"Stock? Purple-hull pea hull stock? Ada Maude. What in the world does it taste like?"

"Well, purple-hull pea hulls, of course, but sweet. You add lots of sugar. And Certo. I found the recipe in a home demonstration pamphlet somebody had left sticking in *Southern Living* at the beauty parlor, and I just thought it sounded like something you'd like. I don't buy peas anymore myself because they give me gas so bad. But all right. I can tell by your tone you don't want to try it." Miss Ada Maude's feelings are hurt, and for a few moments the only sounds are her heels. Then:

"An old man with college football trophies on his mantel like an eighteen-year-old. It was that trip to the Rose Bowl that did it. Ruined him. Pictures in papers all over the country. He never came back down to earth."

"Maybe he did, Ada Maude."

I am watching for Mr. Buddy to come walking home, up Wild Cherry Street. Wild Cherry runs into Connell, right toward the front of my house, so he's a familiar sight to me — walking his route, four times a day, usually, though I've known him to come in and leave again at midmorning and midafternoon. When Bugga's wife died and the café was closed with a wreath on the door, Mr. Buddy just walked back and forth all day for two days. I am remembering how sad it was to me to see him like a lost creature — sadder even than Bugga's wife's death, since she had been ill for years. For a moment I am seeing only Bugga's wife, over three hundred pounds, poor woman.

But now I see Mr. Buddy coming. The crape myrtles are in full bloom all the way down Wild Cherry, ruffly watermelon-pink globes, still heavy from last night's shower, bending the long branches into roman arches over Mr. Buddy. Mr. Buddy is either tipsy or he is weaving to keep his head away from the bees. I watch Mr. Buddy, still nearly three blocks away, as he makes his way toward home and Miss Coralie and Miss Ada Maude.

Mr. Buddy is well over sixty, one of the handsomest men I have ever seen, elegant posture, tall, well groomed, his thick white hair parted and combed. Up close you can see a little mending here and there, a collar turned, but always a crisp white shirt, seersucker suit in the summertime, black and white oxfords, and, ever since I can remember, a straw katy, which he gets out on April 1 and puts away on September 1. I can't imagine where he's gotten them these last years, when men here don't even wear panamas anymore.

His straw katy is Mr. Buddy's chief means of communication on the street, though he is said to talk at the bourée table at night down at Goat's just over the line in Louisiana. If he meets you on the street and he knows you pretty well — as well as he knows me, for instance — he reaches his smooth long-fingered hand up to barely lift the brim of his hat. No big gesture, just the politest little tip, and he says your name: "Jane," he will say to me, or "Miss Effie," or whoever it may be. He doesn't alter his pace, a long, deliberate stride.

When he comes home he walks in the side door — they haven't used the front door for years, since something caused the front porch to settle and the door to stick — and hangs his hat on the hall tree and says, "Coralie," in a very nice tone of voice, and strides to the backstairs and up to his room where, as Miss Ada Maude says, he still has his trophies from an outstanding year at the University of Alabama. I happen to know that Miss Coralie sleeps downstairs in the little room on the other side of the house, where for years she gave me piano lessons. In those days she and Mr. Buddy used to talk.

Even now Miss Coralie takes Mr. Buddy a cup of coffee out on the latticed back gallery early every morning before he puts his tie on. She says, "Have coffee, Buddy?" and he says pleasantly, "Coralie," which seems to include *yes, thank you.*

I am thinking, as I watch Mr. Buddy approach through the watermelon-pink archway like European royalty in an operetta, that he does drink a lot and that he has pulled some tricks over the years while under the influence. My wedding was probably the last social function he attended, fifteen years ago, and when Dr. Whitley solemnly requested that anyone who objected should speak now or forever hold his peace, Mr. Buddy hiccupped so loud you could hear it all over the church. An omen for both of us, maybe. And Mr. Buddy can properly be called trifling, and has been by plenty of others besides Miss Ada Maude, though she is the only person I know who really doesn't like him.

I am also remembering Mr. Buddy's little black rat terrier, Sport, whom he whistled into his car with him, a car he had bought just before the war forced Ford to stop manufacturing automobiles — a V-8 coupé, in which he did considerable damage to light poles, to the car itself, and to other people's cars. It gave up the ghost in the fifties, the same year that Sport, old and deaf, was hit by a delivery truck in front of their house. And I remember how Miss Coralie and I, a child, ran to the little dog while he was still jerking, his eyes glazing, and how she had him taken away so Mr. Buddy wouldn't have to see him like that; she told him that Sport was dead when he walked home for lunch after I had gone home crying.

I am watching Mr. Buddy walking home, lifting his knees high in his way, swinging his arms easily, his head erect. I am waiting for him to catch sight of Miss Ada Maude's baby-blue Continental.

He is alert.

Ah, he sees it. Without interrupting his gait, he makes a U-turn on the walk and heads back to town. He has a problem, now. It is nearly five and he must get home, have a bite of supper, bathe, dress, and be ready for his ride to Goat's when the cardplayers head south.

Miss Ada Maude and Miss Coralie cannot see him, though Miss Coralie must surely have an eye out for him. Miss Ada Maude is saying, "I know you don't like for me to bring this up, but I can't help thinking of how different your life might have been if you'd married Henry George. How he loved you! You could have had everything. Everything, Coralie, if Buddy the great football star hadn't shown up while Henry George was gone offering his life for his country on foreign fields."

"Ada Maude, for pity's sake. Can't we forego the ancient history just this once?"

"Oh, I don't care." There is abandon in Miss Ada Maude's voice. "It's true. Buddy swept you off your feet when you were too young to know what you were doing. And there sits that rich Henry George over there with only one eye, carrying the torch for you to this day." I clap my hand over my mouth at this jumble of images, and I am seeing Miss Ada Maude's upper arm flap its sagging muscle as she waves a hand high over my head toward the shingled tower on Mr. Henry George's mansion.

"Don't be ridiculous, Ada Maude," Miss Coralie is saying. "I never heard of anything so absurd." She is getting weary, thinking she needs to be warming up Mr. Buddy's supper.

"Why are you so loyal to a man who doesn't even talk to you? Just tell me how you feel toward one who is so completely irresponsible, who spends your money, dwells among the lowlife of the town of your birth—he wasn't even born here—and who staggers around smelling like a brewery morning, noon, and night. Do you even know when he comes in at night? How do you even know he is playing cards? Just answer me."

"I'll answer nothing, Ada Maude. You know very well that I am fond of Buddy. He does not stagger. He has his faults . . . He . . . we get along as well as . . ."

"Get along? Get along? Is living your whole life under the same roof with a man who . . . who . . ."

"Just once. Just once. Pees on the courthouse wall?" says Miss Coralie angrily.

"Post office," Miss Ada Maude hisses.

Miss Coralie is going on: "Whether you can understand or not, Sister, I am not an unhappy woman. Think of how many interests I have: I have my music; I cook; I sew; I garden; I read; I'm handy with just about any small tool." I am fearing that Miss Ada Maude is going to be reminded that the last gift Mr. Buddy gave Miss Coralie years ago was a small shovel called a *lady's spade* that he won on a punchboard. "Did you notice I've attached that loose gutter at the corner of the porch? You mentioned it last week."

"You! Up on a stepladder! Oh, Coralie, you are hopeless. Why do I worry so about you? Why don't I give up?"

"Why don't you, Sister?" Miss Coralie's voice is sounding hopeful, friendly.

Now I see Mr. Buddy coming back up Wild Cherry, faster this time. He can see Miss Ada Maude's car but on he comes, and I realize he has no choice but to run the gantlet if he is to play bourée tonight. On he comes, his bearing commanding, courageous. At the corner of Connell, named for his father-in-law, he must stop for a car that passes deliberately and tip his hat. Miss Ada Maude and Miss Coralie are surely seeing him now, Miss Ada Maude bristling, Miss Coralie feeling sorry for him. Up the driveway he walks, past the Continental. His feet are on the steps, and he stamps them as he reaches the high porch to shake off grit from the street.

"Well, Buddy, are we to have the pleasure of your company? Bugga's Café must have closed its doors for the day." I hold my breath. Perhaps her sarcasm will break the great reserve. But of course it does not.

"Ada Maude," he says nicely. "Coralie." He is removing his straw katy.

"Evening, Buddy," says Miss Coralie. The screened door shuts quietly and the sounds of Mr. Buddy's footsteps fade quickly inside the house.

Miss Ada Maude's feet hit the porch floor with her full 160, and she is standing. "He's just too much, Coralie, that man. And you are a fool. You are my sister and I love you. But you have sacrificed your youth to him, and you've martyred yourself for nothing so far as I can see. You could have spent your whole adult life in the finest house in Sweet Bay with a cultured gentleman who would be doting on you to this good day. With all due respect, you *are* a fool."

"You could be right about that, Ada Maude. If it makes you feel any better, sometimes I feel like one."

From the porch Miss Ada Maude calls, "Wake up, Walter." And to Miss Coralie she says, "Just look at that mouth hanging open." Now I hear Walter opening the Continental's door, while Miss Ada Maude is pausing. "You'll never hear another word of any of this from me again, Coralie. Never. Never. Never. And I mean it this time." Her heels thump down seven wood steps.

"See you next Monday," Miss Coralie says, as Walter backs the car into Connell.

I need to go into my own house, begin preparing my own supper. I pick up my abandoned James reader. Here is my chance to move unobserved, to conceal my eavesdropping. But I cannot. I must stay to see Mr. Buddy on his way, back downtown. I am wondering why I should care what they are doing; why I should sit here listening to my neighbors. I have never done such a thing before. Later I will believe that I stayed because I anticipated something—some change in Mr. Buddy's usual departure for Goat's, perhaps.

Mr. Buddy comes back out onto the porch, and I hear him strike a match on the sole of his wing-tipped oxford. Miss Coralie has broken all records tonight. He will get back in time. She, too, is on the porch, and I hear the swing chains' crunch as she says, "Have a nice evening, Buddy."

"Coralie," he says, his tone mellow. I watch him cross Connell and walk down Wild Cherry, tall, straight, dodging the crape myrtle blossoms till he is out of sight.

I sigh and am about to get up when I hear Miss Coralie coming down her steps, quickly, lightly, like a girl. She is humming. She walks toward the back of her place, not more than ten feet from where I sit, my tailbone numb. In the gathering dusk I imagine her slim form, legs swinging in her slacks — her "pants" — her dark hair pulled away from her tanned oval face, her eyes peaceable under her dark graceful eyebrows.

I hear a metallic latch lift, a gate swing, not silently, but not in the rust of neglect. The latch falls. Voices. A man's:

"Sweetheart. You're late. Did Buddy's ride go down late tonight?"

"No, he was delayed. I'm sure they waited for him at Bugga's. They've never left without him. Ada Maude was here so late that poor Buddy couldn't get on in to eat and freshen up."

"Oh. Ada Maude," Mr. Henry George sighs. "It is Monday, isn't it. Why does Ada Maude give Buddy such a hard time after all these years." These were not questions.

Miss Coralie says, "Buddy really got himself into it yesterday."

"I heard," says Mr. Henry George.

"Already?"

"I went to the barber shop this afternoon."

"Oh my. Of course."

"Try not to be upset, Corrie."

"Well, I hate it. Can you imagine a fastidious man like Buddy doing such a thing?"

"He didn't know what he was doing, honey."

"I guess not." Miss Coralie is sounding consoled.

Then they are quiet. Or they do not speak. I can hear them sighing, murmuring, whispering softly. They are embracing. Kissing. I am no longer a mere eavesdropper. I am moving down to voyeur, hoping they do not hear me as I drag the heavy chair back up to the patio behind my house. I go back to unplug my fan.

"I have filets. Do you want me to do them inside or out, darling? Makes no difference to me. I haven't seen any mosquitoes out here." Mr. Henry George sounds so casual.

"Oh . . . let's cook inside tonight." Miss Coralie is walking across Mr. Henry George's patio. I know that they are arm-in-arm as they go into his kitchen, where two thick dark red and perfect filets lie on a cuttingboard. Lettuce is washed, crisping in the refrigerator. Potatoes are oiled by Mr. Henry George's own hands, lovingly, in anticipation.

Lovers. Miss Coralie and Mr. Henry George.

In my own kitchen I am scrounging for some supper, pondering, undecided, staring at the leftovers on the cold shelves of the refrigerator. A chill comes over my face when I open the freezer door. I decide to have a bowl of ice cream. I eat it at my kitchen counter. It is sweet, rich. Delicious. I roll my eyes as a sweet glob slides down my throat, and I wonder and smile as though I am not alone but have someone there to smile back at me. The Water Music changes to the Royal Fireworks, flowing out Mr. Henry George's library window and over the ivied wall that gives me and Mr. Henry George our privacy.

Music Lesson

For two days and nights she had studied the acoustical tiles in the ceiling of the hospital room, trying to decide if they were all alike— poured into a mold of one design. There was no symmetry. Did the small and large decimal points curve and loop in a common pattern? This time she decided they did. And yet . . . For a moment she let her eyes go out of focus and see nothing. She thought, *In God's name, where am I going to get some money?*

The blocks were uneven and poorly installed. He would notice that eventually. Engineer. Perfectionist. He hated slipshod work, and he never accepted any. At a party one night she'd overheard a building contractor call him just another overeducated nitpicking sonofabitch. She'd told him later and he'd laughed.

"Well, what do you think?" he said as he slid the long zipper down her back.

"Well, I don't think you're overeducated." Laughter. "Evan! You're cracking my ribs!" Laughter.

"Let's go to New Orleans and make love all weekend."

"We don't have to go to New Orleans, silly." Laughter. Laughter. What had been so funny?

Nothing had been very funny lately. Notes from those years of fun and laughter sounded in her head, andante—three beautiful children with their clear blue eyes, shining hair, straight, perfect bodies, Easter clothes, vacations at the Gulf Coast, camp, bandaged bobos, and, always, Evan. More real and more recent was the memory of the past year, with conversations ending not in laughter but on strange notes. He'd become irritable, distracted—tired, worried, she now knew—a different Evan who could snap, "I don't see what the hell difference it makes," leaving her cut off and angry. Left to her own lonely thoughts, she'd gradually concluded that a good many things no longer made a hell of a difference—things that had once seemed all important. If only . . .

Her eyes traveled along a fine crack down the pale green wall. The crack disappeared behind the glistening oxygen tent—her husband in a lopsided corsage box. A large machine that seemed primitive hissed beside the bed, reminding her of a window air-conditioning unit. They'd never had a window unit. Only central systems in both the houses they'd built. He hated the sound of a window unit—and the draft. They were inefficient and costly to operate. Better a palmetto fan, he'd said.

She watched the still face. He wasn't unconscious; he was asleep, and he snored gently and naturally. Surely he would not die. He must not. What was his heart doing? A strange red thing, like something from a meat market, throbbing capriciously in his chest, giving life, taking life. The mindless heart, the heartless heart. Her mouth was dry, and her stomach began to feel rigid again. Her breath quickened as she fought the fear that had kept welling up within her since she had come with him into the hospital. The nightmare of the screaming ambulance that whipped them through the streets—streets that flashed by like a hideous kaleidoscope.

She laid her palm up against the wall, looked at the back of her hand, watched the veins disappear and her hand turn creamy and pale, the blood draining down through her wrist, into her arm. She raised her hand higher, above her head, to let the blood run down through her arm and shoulder, into her strong and perfect heart.

During the first few hours she had even hoped Evan's heart attack was a dream. Soon, perhaps, she would wake up and begin to move and feel the cool, smooth sheets of her own bed beneath her, the plump, firm support of her pillow under her shoulders, neck, head. But there was no gasp of relieved awakening, only the numbing insistence of the truth.

Coronary.
Arterial block, ventricular infarction. Fibrillation. She had resisted

the definitions of the ugly words, at first a jumble of confusion and terror in her mind. *Pacemaker.* Very possible, said the cardiologist. How does it work? He had explained that the tiny device would be pushed down through the jugular vein, into a ventricle. But Evan's veins are so small he's never even been able to give a transfusion. My dear, he's stable now. Let's see what happens during the next seventy-two hours. Three days. Two had passed.

She'd left the hospital once, to go home to see about the children. Daddy's going to be all right. While there she discovered, in his mail and in his desk, overdue notices on bank loans and a stack of unpaid bills. A current overdraft notice. The whole story in sixty seconds. The precoronary collection of Evan Phelps. She'd picked up the phone, automatically, and called his secretary. Julia reminded her that her husband's partner was still vacationing in Europe. "I'm sorry, Mrs. Phelps. There just isn't any money on hand. Things couldn't be much worse right now . . . I'm so sorry."

What? What do you mean? But it wasn't Julia's problem.

Now she fingered the textured leather of the prayer book Alice had brought her and stared at the thirty-first Psalm, the page a gray blur. She thought, *I have to have some money. Now. But from where?*

Listen . . . "Moonlight Sonata." "The Scarf Dance." Dvořák, Ravel. "Practice," her mother had said. "You just don't practice enough. You could play as well as your sister, you know." She practiced, but she never played as well as Delia and a lot of other people who were forever having recitals in taffeta dresses, curtsying and smiling to applause, dropping their eyes to proud parents on the front row. She remembered some of her recitals, and felt the first tinge of amusement she'd had in days.

Yet Father gave her the Steinway. Delia had one.

"A house must have a piano," he'd said matter-of-factly. And a typewriter and a few other things — closed bookcases. Dust and Louisiana dampness ruined books and pianos. This before air conditioning.

The doctor had sounded fatherly. "My dear, get Evan some nurses. Go home and get some rest." Go home. She drifted back and forth between the fright of now and the pleasant intrusions of the past.

Delia had once hung a fringed paisley shawl over the piano. The crystal prisms of the lamp shimmered when she played Rachmaninoff. She stared at the unfamiliar stubble on Evan's chin. *Why didn't he tell me about these debts? Why did he let us go on spending?* A few thousand dollars would pay bank interest until the disability insurance started. No, she needed more than that. There were groceries and utility bills.

The doctor had murmured vaguely, "Three months—possibly four, if . . ." *If?*

Three months. *I haven't played in a year,* she thought. I can still read music pretty well. But I couldn't teach; I should have practiced. The piano crowds the living room. But Father said every house . . . Father is dead. Father has been dead for years.

Her candelabra shone in the light of red candles at Christmastime. The parties. The singing. The keyboard gleamed creamy white, like new. The tone, ah. But everyone thinks his piano has a glorious tone. Suddenly she rose from the rumpled cot where she had lain stiffly, listening and watching, for two nights. "I'm going to use the telephone," she said softly to the floor nurse who had come in. "Please stay with him. I'll be right back."

She moved along the polished floor of the long hall. Gleaming reflections swam by her on tile walls, enameled ceiling, lights. An underwater tunnel—as in Mobile. A window would help this place enormously.

The telephone was still warm from the previous user, a tall young black man in a bright blue robe. She wondered what his trouble was; every time she'd wanted to call home he was at the pay phone talking animatedly. To his girlfriend, maybe, telling her about his tests. What the doctor said. The waiting room smelled of fresh paint, and Dutch Boy wet paint signs hung about. The pages of the phone book were curled up at the corners—worn out by people like herself, calling.

"Classified." The voice on the other end startled her.

We used Dutch Boy in our first house. They said it would clean well. It did, too. But the living room was too green. She spoke articulately to the voice, but her head seemed full of ancient things coming on in little waves that would not stop.

"How many lines did you want, ma'am?"

Mother didn't let that scarf stay on the piano for long. She said it was too shiny. The fringe was pale gold and long and silky. Mother's fingers were firm on the keys. Blue veins stood out on her hands, sprinkled with pale freckles, and her engagement ring would turn loosely as she played till the diamond, in a high setting, rattled on the keys. She sat erect, and her right foot always seemed poised above the pedal, her shin standing out. Did Mother really know Liszt? Mother never doubted herself. She just sat down when she pleased and played as she pleased. Then she would get up and go on to other things. Would Mother have panicked if Father had had a heart attack?

"You won't need to say for sale. It will be in that column." A soft voice.

A deep voice. "Every house needs a piano, honey. And a Merriam-Webster." Or Webster-Merriam. Mother ground coffee when she was a little girl on the farm in Copiah County, Mississippi. You couldn't look up at the mill on the wall; coffee got into your eyes. She shut her eyes.

Elise would say, "For heaven's sake. What happened to your piano?" Elise would know, but she'd ask.

Alice would say, "Darling, what a fabulous idea to get rid of that monster. Now you can put in a nice old chest or something." She would know, too. Everyone must know Evan is broke.

He can't die. Oh, God, she thought, what was that Psalm where Alice had laid the ribbon? In Thee, O Lord, do I put my trust. What would he say when he was taken home and saw it was gone? Well, after all, it was her piano. She imagined: "But your piano! How could you do it? Do you realize what it will cost to replace a Steinway?" Replace it? Darling, who needs it?

"How many days do you want to run the ad?"

If I can get two thousand for it, I can manage. I know I can. If I can just get him . . .

"Ma'am, you don't need to say piano; just say Steinway."

Dust motes flew around, going nowhere in the beam of sunlight that struck the piano. *Do re mi fa sol la ti do.* She liked the finish on the metronome better than the piano's. She studied the walnut patina. A bordered Axminster underfoot in the wintertime. In summer the sun glowed on bare polished pine floors, and silk pongee curtains slid lightly on wooden rings and bulged into the room on every breeze. Damp spring air made the keys stick. Mr. Broussard could fix that, but he couldn't play anything. He just sat there with a neat little tool kit open beside him, making chords and cocking his head. On cold winter nights the fire in the coal grate glowed on the dark wood, and the heat caused the piano's finish to craze. It felt rough. Where had father bought it? It had always been there in the living room, like everything else. Mother and Father never bought anything. Mother didn't "decorate." How pretty that grate had been — iron and fancy, glowing as red as the coals. Her shins would smart when she got too close, and she would keep edging back on the rug till the coals burned down.

"Run it for four days, please. Yes, thank you."

It was fun to let her fingers slide off the black keys. Da-dum. Da-dum. The bench had club feet, and dust collected there. She would slip her feet out of her shoes and stretch her legs around to dust them with her toes. When the bench got full of *Etudes,* sheet music, and exercise books, she would go through them and clean it out, so the top would fit down properly. Mother hated edges of music sticking out.

"Bill me." She gave the address and hung up the clammy green receiver, its metal cord coiling instantly, snakelike. As she turned away the phone rattled. Her coin had come back.

She started down the hall to his room. *What if no one wants to buy it? Can I sell it for less? No, I won't give it away.* She avoided the green tiles, stepping only on the white. Her shoes were nearly the length of the squares. She stopped. A puddle of dark blood larger than a dinner plate lay on the floor. Two attendants were rolling an empty stretcher with rumpled green sheets out of a room. One man stepped back into the blood, then they pushed the stretcher toward the elevator, leaving heelprints of somebody's blood on the floor. She moved past, her hand clutching the coin in her pocket. Jamie said you could see Lincoln's statue between the columns of the memorial when a penny was new. Was he kidding?

Passing the nurses' station, she looked at each face apprehensively.

All of them returned her nervous smile with benign, noncommittal stares, much like the squares of ivory tiles behind them. But the nurses had been kind. They saw women like her every day, scared-faced women having their first crisis, their emotions moving between calm and panic.

Silently she pushed the heavy door open and nodded the waiting nurse out. Evan's eyes were open, watching her till she stood beside him. He put his hand out and pulled her hand into the cold tent and kissed her fingers with cold lips. "I was just wondering something." His voice sounded—thin.

"I was just wondering how many miles you and I have danced together."

Laughter hung in her throat. "About a million miles—so far."

"How are the kids? The nurse said you were at the phone."

"They're fine. Jean and Delia are coming to see you—in a few days—and Jamie says to tell you he's moving into his tree house till you come home." They smiled. She tucked his hand under the sheet and sealed the edges of the tent with the sheet as she had seen the nurses and doctors do. She stood looking at him as he closed his eyes again.

You'd never dream what I've done.

She sat down on the cot and leaned back against the hard wall. She was disappointed to feel the pang of resentment. She'd hoped she wouldn't. It lasted barely long enough for her to recognize it. Then it was gone, like a ghost that didn't wait around to be exorcised. The piano would sell. Several burly men would come, turn it on its side, take it out the front door, and lay it in a van on quilted pads. Then they would come back for the legs and their screwdriver. The big brass casters would leave three packed-down places in the carpet, but she was confident that a good brush and a little time would restore the pile.

The Painter

I wonder what difference it might have made if Mrs. Heaslip had not come upon us that day long ago. It was summer and we were eight, Wesley and I. We lay on our stomachs, the sidewalk hurting our hipbones. In the shade of Mrs. Heaslip's Chinese elms Wesley drew pictures with the softest rocks he could find in his driveway — human faces in profile.

"You, Wesley! You, Laura! Marking up my sidewalk again!" I can see Mrs. Heaslip's fat ankles overhanging her black kid ties near my face, her shoestrings with soft, silky tassels, black georgette curtaining her bulk in a wide circle, wafting Hinds Honey and Almond Cream and Cashmere Bouquet talcum. As she stood over us her tone changed. "Why, Wesley! That's remarkable, honey." Shifting her weight from side to side, she rocked heavily into her house. Soon she came out, let herself down onto the glider on her screened porch, and laid a Sears catalog over her knees. She licked her thumb. *On a hill far away* . . . she began to rumble softly as she turned the pages. That could be how it all began for Wesley Rimes. I'm not sure. But two weeks later she handed him a complete oil paint set, saying, "I ordered you something." And he went home to become a painter.

That same summer it was Wesley who was first waked up before daylight by a red glare flickering on the sleeping-porch wall, and he shook Rembert not knowing that it was the Galloways' house on fire. Rembert tore himself out of bed, yelling, "Fire! Fire! Fire!" and while he ran across the street and was pulling the Galloways out their side door, Mrs. Rimes cranked the phone, shouting, "Birdie! Birdie! Wake up Frank Buie! The Galloways' house is afire!"

All of us, young and old, began to come out into Wild Cherry Street in summer nightclothes. Frank Buie started up the siren and the bell on the firetruck at the other end of the street. It was all something to stay in a child's mind.

Mrs. Rimes pulled a rocking chair off her front porch. "Sit down, Mamie," she said, as she put a coat around Mrs. Galloway. Mrs. Galloway sat on the Rimeses' lawn in the rocking chair, her thin gray hair in kid curlers, her hands working in her lap, and watched her house blacken and fall in on itself in the red flames that scorched our faces. Her eyes shining in the glare, she stared and mourned the loss of her engagement ring, left on her dressing table, and the dutch-girl quilt, just finished, that lay in the downy ashes of her cedar chest. Mr. Galloway had saved his dentures.

Wesley pressed himself against the Rimeses' side porch, the edge of the floor just above his head. "Aren't you cold, son?" asked Hardy Pell, the town printer. Wesley wore a cotton nightshirt, his thin legs bare, his teeth chattering. He said nothing, and the fire burned in his pupils. Hardy patted his shoulder. "Come by my shop tomorrow. I'll make you some more drawing pads." But Wesley only stared at the fire. I remember even now, fifty years later, his child's features, softly drooping lids over large eyes, round cheeks, full lower lip, gentle puff under his chin.

My father shouted, "Frank, throw some water on my roof. Aubrey's house is gone. Those flying sparks . . ." We children, shivering, watched till the red glare of fire gave way to the pale, foggy dawn.

I remember when he was about ten Wesley Rimes began to mow the lawns of nearby neighbors to earn money for his painting supplies. Early on a summer morning his mower made a gentle clatter, and to me, lying in bed, it sounded like a cowbell far out in a meadow. The dew-wet grass flew in a small green blizzard and stuck to his tennis shoes, ankles. With his fan-shaped bamboo rake Wesley heaped the grass cuttings into neat cones around the shrubbery. Then he took the huck towel that hung from his back pocket and wiped his face and neck. Having finished, he would turn his mower over and pull it easily behind him. As he walked home the blades turned idly, ineffectually, and the metal wheels bumped over mounds of bermuda grass in cracks of the sidewalk. He stored the mower in their garage along with his oil can, tools, a coil of rope, a ladder, odds and ends. They had no car, but I remember the wide oil-stained planks implanted in the gravel, tracks for the car they had owned when Wesley's father was alive.

By the time he was a teenager Wesley painted most of the time. He seemed to stop only long enough to earn a dollar or two to buy more paint and canvas. When he talked to Rembert about his painting, Rembert would look up from his solitaire or his crossword puzzle and say, "Yeah, Wes," or "That's great, Wes." Evelyn, his sister, would shake her head and say, in her delicate, clear voice, "How do you do it, Wesley? I can't draw a straight line."

Mrs. Heaslip pointed to the panel of faded pastel pansies over the sideboard. "Just look at that. He gets it from you, Lois. I never heard of any of the Rimeses having this kind of talent, did you?"

"Oh, Idabelle, I did that so long ago . . ." It was true, Mrs. Rimes had painted in pastels and watercolor herself before teaching became a full-time job. Widowhood had borne heavily upon her, and only in the pursuit of survival did she display any enthusiasm — thrift, frugality, survival. If she seemed not to show warmth to her children or her pupils, it was probably because she felt lonely in her responsibilities. This in turn produced a sort of lonely detachment in Rembert and Evelyn and Wesley.

Mrs. Rimes's small keen features were surrounded by networks of fine taut lines, and her bright eyes were apprehensive beneath a gray tumbleweed of hair where a hairpin or two swung. Her fine-boned figure was long ago lost in dumpy shapelessness. In summer she conducted Latin and mathematics classes around her dining room table. Lagging pupils grumbled at her demands, but for forty years she was known for pulling the least promising up to passing.

After Evelyn was graduated from high school she got a job selling cosmetics at the Blue Tile Pharmacy. The drugstore's cater-cornered entrance at Railroad Avenue and Main Street was faced and floored with small hexagonal blue tiles. Back when Mr. E. J.

Silkensted set up his drugstore, his heavy safe was dropped on the floor in front of the door, cracking and chipping the tiles. The rough spot annoyed ladies in high heels, but it never cost Mr. Silkensted any business because he had the only drugstore in town. Evelyn Rimes sold cosmetics to help pay her way through college. The shy girl sampled fragrant creams and powders from Mr. Silkensted's glass cases, trying to cover the large strawberry birthmark on her cheek. But she had to put the makeup on so heavily that it dried and cracked like stale pudding, so she left her birthmark bare, and people were hardly aware of it.

Wesley Rimes grew up painting in his studio. Originally a pantry, it was lighted by a big north window. The walls were of narrow tongue-in-groove pine, dark. An unshaded electric light hung from the ceiling, a flat switch on the socket to turn it on. He had a wrought-iron bridge lamp with an ecru accordion-pleated shade that Mrs. Martin gave him for helping her move two large cape jasmines from either side of the Galloway steps to either side of her own front steps. The lamp had a flexible neck that enabled Wesley to focus the light on his easel at night. He painted portraits of people about the town. A few, framed in pretentious gilt, hung in rosewood and velvet parlors, commanding a whole room with terra-cotta flesh and bright hard eyes with the whites too white. Wesley put a careful dab of white zinc on the pupils for highlight and beside that a small fleck of crimson lake. The paintings were primitive and harsh, marvelously bad, and remarkable likenesses.

Mrs. Charles Nichols had Wesley paint a portrait of her son, Charles, Jr. Her son was talked about for his wildness, and he was seldom at home. From semester to semester the Nicholses' friends did not know where Charles, Jr., was in school. Vanderbilt? Tulane? Sunflower Junior College? He took flying lessons and flew his own little plane low over the courthouse, where he dispatched several rolls of toilet paper that unfurled in flimsy tangles over the trees, box hedges, and over the statue of his grandfather.

He was "a drunk," "oversexed," and he "slept with niggers." Such a legend, Wesley hoped, could be painted from life in helmet and goggles, with a white silk scarf at his throat. But Mrs. Nichols gave him several photographs to work from, and Wesley painted a stark, stiff pose that had a posthumous look about it. I thought that if Charlie were killed in his airplane, the portrait could be run at the top of his obituary in the Jackson paper, and the eyes would have that look. When Wesley delivered the portrait to Mrs. Nichols she met him at her front door and gave him a crisp ten-dollar bill for his work, more than he had ever been paid. He carried it home in his hand all the way up Wild Cherry Street, and let me hold it for a moment. "Don't wrinkle it," he said seriously.

Some time later Wesley and I took some dresses to Mrs. Nichols that his mother had altered. Rotella let us in and took us into the breakfast room and gave us some warm cookies with hot, soft raisins in them.

"Miz Neva be right back," she said. "She run down to the Emporium to get me some wax. You-all just wait."

"Where'd you-all hang the portrait I painted of Charlie?"

"Huh? I don't know nothing about that. You-all look around all you please. But I ain't seed no new pitcher nowhere." As she went back into the kitchen she added, "And I wouldn't bother with no painting of that rascal."

We went into the big living room, Wesley's eyes searching the walls. He stood in front of the mantel and looked at the large print of a girl in a bonnet with pink ribbons that seemed to be blowing lightly in a breeze.

"That's *Pinky*. But I guess you know that." Mrs. Nichols had come silently into the room on the soft carpet. "Isn't she lovely?"

"Yes, ma'am. Is she somebody in your family? Who painted her?"

Mrs. Nichols laughed. "No, Wesley. This is from a very famous painting by Thomas Lawrence. This child, by the way, was the aunt of Elizabeth Barrett Browning. Laura, I bet you knew that." She looked briefly my way, as if to acknowledge her faith in my scholarship.

"Mrs. Nichols, have you hung my portrait of Charlie?"

"What? Oh, no. No, not yet, Wesley. I haven't got it framed yet. I meant to take it with me to New Orleans last week, but . . ." She pressed her thin knobby fingers against her cheek. Blue veins lay over the little chicken bones on the back of her hand. Abruptly she walked to the bookcase. "Now, Wesley, you take this big art book home with you and keep it as long as you want to. It's just full of gorgeous color prints of some of the world's greatest paintings." She walked us to the front door. "Thank you for bringing the dresses. Bye bye, Laura. Oh, wait! I almost forgot." She hurried away and returned with three dollars to pay his mother.

Some days Wesley would walk along the topsy-turvy sidewalks of the town. The roots of oaks, bays, magnolias, and wild cherries that lined the streets raised whole squares of concrete and broke up others, and Wesley said to me that he felt there was great power in the roots as he stepped over them. They might come out of the ground and wrap around you like the boa constrictor we saw in the peeling circus poster on Mr. Hiram Kennedy's barn. In his studio Wesley made drawings of the town, but he was never able to evoke the subtle color and texture of roots or the flaky gray-green patches of moss that spread over them.

The sight that Wesley Rimes painted over and over was the remains of the Galloway house. The foundation sat like a great black table, its dull red chimneys high-backed chairs on either side. The front steps were still in place. In spring and summer Wesley's pictures showed only a hint of the charred floor, with tall grasses and lush weeds growing about it. Virginia creeper climbed the chimneys shaded by pecan trees under blue skies. Or he painted it on stormy days with all the greenery glistening in the rain. After frost the vines and grasses would turn brown and brittle and drop away, and the towhees would peck around in the dry litter. Then Wesley painted brick piers naked, bare chimneys, the sky white through gray veils of leafless trees.

Wesley Rimes never tired of making new versions of the Galloway place. When he was about eighteen he showed his pictures to Hardy Pell, who had not forgotten the face of the small boy staring at the burning house. "Don't ever throw these away, Wesley," he said. "Give them to me, if you don't want them. I'll save them for you, and one day they'll mean a lot to somebody."

No one had ever spoken to Wesley of preserving his work. He was so grateful that he painted Hardy Pell's portrait and gave it to him. He showed the printer with bright pink clay skin, his shock of gray hair hanging over his forehead like Spanish moss. It made me think of Moss Hill south of town except for the eyes — pure Prussian blue, which was the only tube of blue that Wesley had at the time — highlighted with a dab of zinc. A small crimson point burned in the pupils.

"Well, would you look at that!" said Hardy Pell. "Well, I declare, now. That was mighty nice of you, Wesley. Much obliged." But when he took it home, his wife said it did not look like her husband, and she did not like the eyes of a stranger following her. Hardy hung it in his printing office behind the letterpress. He never cleaned up his shop, so it became coated with dust and draped with cobwebs. But the eyes burned through.

In his early twenties Wesley Rimes began to have spells of melancholy. The Great Depression was at its worst, and he told me that he contributed nothing to the family's upkeep. He walked the tortured sidewalks of the town, his hands deep in his pockets, his shoulders hunched. He would go back to his studio and try to paint. He found a job helping Mr. Colley Wolfe stack lumber, but a large splinter got into Wesley's hand the first day and festered so he had to stop. Then Mr. Colley had to give the job to his son-in-law, who was laid off by the highway department.

With whitewash Wesley painted footprints on the sidewalk leading to Trellis Fortinberry's dry goods store to advertise Trellis's annual back-to-school sale. "I used to could do this myself," said Trellis, holding his lower back with both hands. Some merchants watched, and when Wesley rose from his knees, Trellis paid him one dollar.

Wesley tried other jobs. He became more depressed. His mother's nine-month teaching salary was cut to sixty dollars per month, and Rembert was working only half a day at the post office. Evelyn waited tables at the state college for women to pay her senior-year tuition and board, but Mrs. Rimes shook her head over Evelyn's chances to stay.

One day Wesley sat down heavily in the cane-bottomed chair beside the rolltop desk in Hardy Pell's printing shop and began to talk. He told the printer about black thoughts that would not go away. "I can't explain it," he said. "I don't sleep good anymore, and when

I do, I wake up with a scared feeling in my stomach. I feel like I'm no good for anything. What good is painting? It used to mean everything to me. But now it seems like — nothing. I'm not a good painter, and what if I was . . . ? I've got to earn some money to help Mama."

"Wait, Wesley," said Hardy when the young man rose and turned to leave. "That's the longest speech I ever heard you make." They walked to the screen door together. "You mustn't let your money worries get you down. Lord, we're all in the same boat. Now, listen, I want to look into one of those W.P.A. projects for you. I've read about artists getting jobs painting murals and all sorts of pictures in federal buildings — post offices. Some of them are unknown painters like you, who need work. Let me look into it for you. I'll write the letter this afternoon."

I was in the kitchen with Mrs. Rimes that afternoon when Wesley came in and told her what Hardy Pell was doing for him. A shaft of sunlight shot through the screened door before him, and there were signs of a lift about him — his shoulders, his dark straight eyebrows. He looked at his mother's eyes and smiled. I remember how Mrs. Rimes laid down the big slotted spoon and turned away from the stove. "It would just be too good to be true," she said. Later, when Wesley showed her and his brother and me a copy of the letter that Hardy wrote, they were pleased. Mrs. Rimes smiled, and she wrote to Evelyn. Soon Hardy produced a reply to his letter stating that Wesley should be getting inquiries, perhaps even an interview. Wesley brought the letter across the street to my porch where we sat and looked at it, and I speculated extravagantly on what the future held for him.

At the post office Rembert watched for a letter for his brother, and Wesley listened for Rembert's step on the porch each afternoon. After several months, Wesley Rimes's despondency returned and took full possession of him. He lay in his bed, facing the faded wallpaper. He did not paint, and his palette, uncleaned, dried to a crust, a hopeless glob of color that held fast his palette knife and a brush. I went over to his house and found him lying on his bed. I said, "Wesley . . . ?" He clamped his dark lashes down, and when they began to glisten I thought he would talk or reach for my hand, which I laid on his shoulder. But he didn't speak or move.

"Artists must suffer," my father shrugged. "It's more than that," I said.

One night soon after that, his mother watched him step out into the summer air that throbbed with living noises—frogs, crickets, and, on porches, people talking, their swings squeaking. "Wesley," she called. "Son?" But he did not turn, and she saw him disappear down Wild Cherry Street. Somewhere, as he trudged the familiar faults of the sidewalks beneath the trees of the town, I know that he surrendered to the power of the roots.

Early the next morning my father stood in the Rimeses' garage with Mr. Hollis Martin and Dr. Bierce, who was coroner then. The garage looked as it always did, now that Frank Mooney had come in his hearse-ambulance and carried Wesley's body away—the strange remnant, neck broken, eyes and tongue protruding. Only Rembert, Dr. Bierce, Hardy Pell, and my father saw. But their descriptions became irresistible phrases picked up and repeated.

Dr. Bierce shifted his cigar. "You see, he climbed up to the rafter on this old ladder and put the rope around his neck. The old rope gave way later, I guess, and that's why he was on the ground when Rembert found him. They had waited up for him all night. Then about daylight Rembert, he . . ."

"God Almighty," Mr. Hollis said.

My father said, "We haven't had a suicide here since old lady Coughlin drank iodine back about '25 or '26."

"It was '24," said Dr. Bierce. "Ten years ago, Will."

"God Almighty," said Mr. Hollis, looking from the rafter to the gravel floor of the garage. My father told us all this later and said that he feared Mr. Hollis might have one of his angina attacks.

That day a kind of shudder seemed to pass in and out of the houses as the news spread, early. By nine o'clock everyone in town had heard about it. Mrs. Heaslip said, "Why, I just spoke to the child a few days ago and he seemed—normal." Her chin all but disappeared into two great soft creamy collars of flesh as she bowed her head and wept into a hemstitched handkerchief.

At the Rimeses' home she and Miss Ivette received the callers who came and went all day and some who sat up all night with the body.

The concerned people of the town who always attended to sad matters sat around the living room talking in quiet voices.

"Whatever made him do it?"

Aunt Teenie Murrell stood in the doorway, a bouquet of her own small red roses in her hand. "The Lord works in mysterious ways, his wonders to perform. I'll just go back and find a small vase in Lois's kitchen." Her steps tapped down the hall, muffled by the threadbare runner.

"I just never knew this boy very well. I mean . . . I saw him . . ."

"Sometimes he would look right through you, like he didn't see you."

"He spoke to me last week. I was coming out of Trellis's. Went in there for some shoes. Did you get to his summer's-end sale?"

"What did he say?"

"I don't remember. You know, you don't remember things like . . ."

I breathed shallowly trying not to be sick and wondering why florist flowers smell of death and home-grown ones smell of life.

Aunt Teenie set her roses on the mantel in a syrup pitcher. Their limp, spiny little necks hung over the rim, their petals open like the mouths of Della Robbia choristers. "The Lord has called his lamb home," she said and settled her small, aged body into the wicker rocker next to the coffin.

"It's too bad he couldn't get the W.P.A. job."

"What job?"

"Painting pictures in post offices, or something like that. Hardy's been trying to help him."

"I didn't know Lois's boy painted. I thought he worked at the post office."

"That's the other one—Rembert."

"Ah."

"I'm so proud of the portrait he did of Charles, Jr., several years ago. I'm going to get that out and have it framed." Mrs. Nichols touched her short snowy curls, removed her rimless pince-nez from the permanently pinched-up bridge of her nose. She reeled the glasses in to her bosom with a small flourish and leaned over to me. "It will be a collector's item now, Laura. I said to Charlie, 'poor marvelous boy'—of course Charlie didn't know what I meant. And poor Miss Lois. Why, Honey, she taught me Latin over thirty years ago." She reeled her glasses out again and clamped them on her nose and peered at her little platinum watch, its face cluttered with roman numerals and wreathed in a crust of diamonds.

The green scroll on the edge of the carpet curled back and forth like an amiable snake beneath twenty pairs of crossed and comfortable ankles. The eyes of the mourners roved to the closed gray coffin that sat in the bay window under a spray of white carnations and dark green fern. From the floor an oscillating fan conducted the company with dependable and solemn rhythm, stirring fern fronds and dress hems.

The Rimes family was shut away in Mrs. Rimes's bedroom. Hardy Pell sat late at his rolltop desk with a bottle of illegal liquor and stared into a pigeonhole, black and deep and empty.

Lucky Lafe

Me and Lafe had a few snorts together last night — first time in about a year. Seems like it gets harder and harder to get together. We'll go along, running into each other at the bank or the gas station almost every day. One of us will say, "Let's get together. Soon, now." And we keep putting it off. Well, last night we made it, and Lafe told me the story again — like only Lafe can tell it. I tell you, if I was a writer, I'd put it all down. Not just because it's a great story, but because of the way Lafe tells it. He ain't overdramatic, just cool, and he talks for his mother and Joel and the fellows at the pool hall just like he was in a play. Only it's not just a tale. It's all true. And even after all these years, when he gets to the part where Joel goes home to tell their mother, I get goose bumps. I'm not too old to get goose bumps.

We were at the big round table in his mama's old dining room last night, his now, with the light over the middle. The fireplace in there is in a corner, with a fancy wood mantel, and the fire was flickering on the wainscot and on the old sideboard with the brown marble top. The apples shined on the sideboard just like when Mrs. Carvel polished them with the purple tissue paper that apples used to come wrapped in. A great room for a few drinks and some talk. Cozy. Nobody but me and Lafe. Corinne was in New Orleans visiting her sister.

Lafe's hair is gray — almost white — but still thick, and he parts it just the same. I'm just about bald. We grew up together from the time we were babies, and I figure I couldn't have had a better friend.

But the story. The story is about Lafe and his mother and his brother in World War II. Me and Lafe — that is, Lafe and I — we wanted to be pilots, but I went in the army and Lafe in the navy. I never did get out of the country, but it seemed to me like Lafe was out in the Pacific before you could say Jack Robinson, and on an aircraft carrier. He was a seaman first class. We sent our pictures home about the same time, and our mothers got together and carried on over us — me with my PFC chevron showing up plain and Lafe in his funny little sailor suit — too tight looking — and with that little white cap jammed down on his ears. That handsome guy resembled this actor Paul Newman, but he looked more like a big-eared monkey in that sailor outfit.

I went over to Camp Shelby and then on to Hood, and then I was up at Meade when the war was over — VE Day and then VJ Day. I never did get overseas. Hell, who cares now? Who even remembers? But I still wish I had got some kind of overseas duty — somewhere — something to tell my kids about. Not that kids have much interest in World War II, specially mine, being girls. Anyway, I was just another stateside private.

But never mind all that. Lafe went to San Francisco and was put on this aircraft carrier right off the bat. Listen, did you ever see one of those things? God, it was bigger than two or three football fields — he said you could hardly see from one end to the other.

They'd been fooling around the Pacific three or four weeks, out somewhere close to — oh, I forget which one of those islands where there was so much rough stuff about that time. It was a real hot spot, but they were just slipping along on the blue water. They knew there were Japs in those parts, so everyone had been kinda jumpy, but actually, says Lafe, they were having a pretty good time — no action. They did their everyday jobs, played some cards, and had good eats — there are thousands of guys on those carriers. Then on a Tuesday they were all going about their business when the radar picked up one little old plane, way off. Well, the old man got on his horn, and everybody hustled to their posts and waited and watched, and pretty soon sure enough, here it come. A Jap fighter, homing in. But wait. It couldn't be no ordinary plane — just one brave little bastard coming right on at them all by himself.

"Sonofabitch!" hollers Lafe to his dub. "It must be a goddam kamikaze!" They shielded their eyes against the high-up sun and watched that little speck way up there. Everybody was froze — except the gunners, and the Jap was too little to hit, it seemed like. He circled around once or twice like a buzzard spotting a field mouse. Then *zoom*.

"Here it comes. Straight down," hollered Lafe's buddy. Lafe always gets his voice quieter when he tells about any shouting or excitement. And down it come, on a beeline for the elevator amidships.

"Jesus," Lafe hollered and over the side he went — just in the nick of time. That crazy little Jap come right on down and blew a huge hole in the guts of the ship. But it didn't break in two or sink like you'd expect. Too big, I guess.

All hell broke loose — explosions one after the other, red-hot fires, black smoke, yelling and screaming, guys blinded, and stuff falling on the deck and in the water. Lafe was blown way off into the ocean but, crazy as it may sound, he wasn't hurt. See? This is what I mean about him. He came up, feeling a little crazy at first, but he treaded water, and before long he swam a ways and caught hold of a life jacket. The sea was right smooth and he just held on there, and pretty soon it was late afternoon and the ship was out of sight.

"Man. What'd you do then, Lafe?" I always ask.

"I took a leak," Lafe always answers. That's part of the story. I don't know whether he did or not, but I think about it nice and warm on him for a minute like it used to be over in Hanley's Creek where the water was ice cold.

Before dark, a U.S. plane come along and swooped down low. Lafe, he waved. They took a couple of low swipes and dropped a raft practically on top of him, full of supplies. Lafe climbed aboard — plum wore out, for godsake. Lord knows how he made it over the side. He just flopped down exhausted and waterlogged. Course, many's the time he and I treaded water in Hanley's Creek practically all day long. But that was different. For one thing we could find the bottom if we wanted to, and for another there weren't any sharks to nip our bare asses in Hanley's. It's a wonder a shark didn't get Lafe out there in the ocean before he could get into that raft. But that's old Lafe for you—lucky. Always. He beat anything I ever heard of.

He won all our marbles when we were kids. Then he'd give them back and win them again. When we moved on to craps, same thing. He could roll a seven right off the bat, or make his point. Anything he wanted, there it come. He won eighty dollars at Bank Night at the Majestic, and he won a radio on a punchboard at the Standard filling station.

I knew Lafe'd go far and he did. He's a lawyer now, practices right here in Sweet Bay. Folks have tried to get him to run for judge. Not Lafe. He's been too good at this corporation law all over the state to mess up the Carvel name in politics. They're into their fifth generation here.

Funny thing about Lafe's name. His daddy, Judge Franklin Carvel, named him for a writer that Lafe's grandpa knew way back there. I've heard the Judge tell it a hundred times. He'd stand there and drop his pinch-nose glasses in his breast pocket. "I named my boy for Lafcadio Hearn, the New Orleans writer. My father and he were friends when Father was a medical student at Tulane. Hearn was a strange sort—he went on to Japan, where he became a great man of letters. A great man. Yessir. He and Father corresponded." Just like that. Judge kept one of Lafcadio Hearn's letters to Doc in his safe.

Doc Carvel, Lafe's granddaddy, was a great old family doctor— went out on house calls any time of night. Mama says he'd come and mop out her throat with silver nitrate at two o'clock in the morning if Mamaw called him. But Old Doc was one of them quiet, lonely drinkers and that's what finally got him, they say. All I can remember about him is he wore black soft-looking high-top shoes, and he sat on his porch at night in a wicker rocker, still in his tie and coat, even in the summertime. He seemed old to me, and I guess he was.

Judge called Lafe *Lafcadio* because he knew how special this Lafcadio bird was to Old Doc, but Lafe's mama took pity on him and called him Lafe like the rest of us did. Lafe didn't give a hoot, I can tell you. He didn't resent a name like Lafcadio. Not Lafe. Every now and then somebody'd give him a little static about it. I can remember one time in particular. Herb Jones, whose full name is

Herbert Chichester Jones (his mother was one of the Chichesters),
waltzed up to Lafe — we were about ten at the time — and just bawled
out for no reason at all, "Mr. Lafcadio Hearn Carvel," in a loud
voice right out in the middle of Railroad Avenue.

Lafe, he never turned a hair. He just grinned at old Herb and said,
"Whatcha want, Mr. Herbert Chickenshit Jones?" And that ended
it so far as Lafe was concerned. But Mrs. Jones rang up Mrs. Carvel
to tell on Lafe and then realized she couldn't say *chickenshit* over
the phone to Mrs. Carvel, so she ended up with, "Well, Mary Nell,
I suggest that you wash Lafe's mouth out with soap. I'm not the
only one that knows he has a naughty tongue, and I just don't want
him polluting Herbie's mind."

Lafe was lucky with girls, too. He got all the best ones, or worst,
whichever he was looking for, when we were in high school. Louise
Dobbs — Easy Louisey — Lafe was going out with her on what we
called late dates when, bless goodness, she turned up expecting.
Before you could say pea turkey, Buddy Galloway steps up to Brother
Higginbotham down at the Baptist parsonage with her. Nowadays
she's president of the garden club, and Buddy's superintendent of
the Sunday school — Methodist. They — but who gives a damn about
Louise and Buddy. I'm just saying Lafe was too smart *and* lucky
to of married her and had that boy that turned out to be the spittin'
image of old Buddy Galloway. But Buddy is stupid enough to of
married her and had a boy who could've looked like Lafe. See what
I mean?

Well, there was old Lafe, sunning himself in a life raft a million
miles from nowhere. Didn't know where he was and says he never
worried a minute. To this day I think it's a crying shame I couldn't
of been there with him.

Back home the War Department got busy. I think the telegram
said "missing and presumed lost," or something about that hopeless. Poor Mrs. Carvel. Judge had died by then. Joel was fifteen.
He and Lafe were all she had left, and she had a bad heart. Mama
said Mrs. Carvel was brave, but Berteal, their cook, told Mama she
cried when Joel wasn't in the house. Thought sure Lafe was dead.
What else could she think? The aircraft carrier disaster was in all
the papers and on the radio with lists of dead, missing, and injured;

descriptions of bodies picked up in the ocean. All that. It seemed sure that if he was "missing" from that mess, he wasn't out there walking on water. So she knew he was dead.

Dead? Lafe? Are you kidding? Not that lucky rascal. Listen to this. There was a whole row of screwups in communications. In the first place, he didn't even know the navy had him down as missing. He went through about three hospitals to be thumped over and to rest; papers got mixed up. Mrs. Carvel was home grieving, and old Lafe was resting his way right back to the west coast.

Almost a month after the telegram came, Lafe got off the train in Sweet Bay. You wonder why he never dropped his mama a card? So did she, but she never labored the point. That was just Lafe — *was* Lafe. Not now, of course. Not after he finished his education — got to be a lawyer and married Corinne. Corinne straightened him out good. He calls her if he's going to be five minutes late to supper. He married her in New Orleans after he finished law school. Corinne is all right. Folks big dogs in New Orleans society and rich as Croesus, and they loved Lafe. But Corinne is plain as an old shoe and tight as a tick. Why, that girl will — but this story ain't about Corinne.

I wish I'd a been there that day when Lafe got home. Me and Lafe have always been close, even though we've gone different ways at times. I didn't go to college after the war like he did, but that never has made any difference to Lafe. I married Mary Eunice — now she went to Ole Miss — and took over her daddy's gin — had lint in my eyebrows ever since, and money in the bank, too, if you want to know the truth. Own a few cattle, nice little bass pond. No reason for Mary Eunice and Corinne to be as close as Lafe and me, but they know we're going to get together a few times a year to hunt or fish or, like last night, just sit around the table and have a few drinks and shoot the bull. Every year or so he tells me the story again. He knows how I love to hear it, I guess, because I don't think he talks about it anymore to anybody else.

Lafe stepped off Number 3 that afternoon and stood there on the gravel while the train eased on off to Jackson. When the last car rolled past he could see across the tracks, through the bay trees in Railroad Park, and there was Railroad Avenue big as life. He hopped those double tracks same as he had before any of us ever heard of Hitler or Hirohito. He ducked under the scrawny privet arbor and crossed the street like he hadn't just returned from being blown off an aircraft carrier by a suicide plane. He grinned at a few dumbfounded folks — everybody knew Lafe — and he headed into the pool hall. The pool hall was in a vacant store that Old Man Reeder owned then. His daughter rents it out to a chain store now. Dime store.

Who do you think was all drawed back and ready to make a shot at the middle table? Joel Carvel. His back was to the door. The draft hadn't left many able-bodied pool shooters in Sweet Bay, but those who were there that day thought they were seeing a ghost when Lafe walked in. Joel knew something was going on behind his back. He laid his cue down on the green baize table and turned around. Slow-like. The afternoon sun was behind Lafe, and Joel couldn't make him out at first. He cocked his head to one side and squinted. Then Lafe came toward him and grinned, and somebody finally found his tongue and sputtered, "Christ."

I wish I could of been there. Joel grabbed Lafe and hugged him and cried. Right there. He didn't care who saw him. Everybody crowded around, pounding Lafe, shaking his hand. Lucky Lafe. Lucky Lafe. At first Lafe never realized they'd thought he was dead.

"Wait a minute," says Joel, and he took a swipe at his eyes with his sleeve. "Mama! Lord, I gotta get home and break this to her easy. She's been half-crazy over you dying. Now I gotta tell her you're alive. Man, this is liable to kill her." You could've heard Lafe laugh all the way up at the drugstore. Then he got serious, because they finally got it through his head that his mother really did think he was dead. She had to be handled right or she might have a heart spell.

"Look, Lafe," says Joel, "We gotta get home to Mama 'fore somebody calls her from downtown and gives it to her the wrong way. I bet Miss Ida saw you from the café window. If she did, you know she's already on the phone." Lafe knows Sweet Bay, and he says, "Come on, Joel, let's cut out the back through the alley."

They ran, says Lafe — raced each other all the way — and made it in three minutes. On the front porch Lafe leaned against the post and got his breath before he followed Joel into the house.

Mrs. Carvel was back in the kitchen.

"Mama?"

"Yes, Joel? What is it, Honey? You all right?"

"Mama?"

"Joel? What's the matter with you? Is something wrong?"

"No, Mama. Nothing's wrong."

"Well, what'd you come running in here like that for, Son?"

"Mama, how—how'd you like to hear some good news, for a change?"

"Good news? Joel, you're all the good news I've got left."

"No, Mama. You shouldn't have given up on Lafe. I mean, I think he's alive. Lafe is alive. I never believed he was dead, Mama. He's alive."

"Joel." She put her arm around him. "Darling, what's made you run in here like this, so full of hope? Bless your . . ."

"Mama, sit down. It's true. I'm trying to tell you. I've got word. Don't get too excited now."

"Got word? Joel . . ." Now her voice was a whisper, and she clutched his sleeve and looked close at his face.

"He's alive, Mama."

"In a hospital? Hurt? Bad?"

"No. There was a mixup. He's perfectly OK."

"Oh, Joel. Lafe! Is Lafe alive? Is he coming home?" She was crying now and shaking.

"He *is* home."

"You mean in the States?"

"I mean in the dining room, Mama." And he pushed open the swinging door.

"Lafe!"

And there stood old Lafe in front of the sideboard, grinning, with his arms stretched out wide to his mama.

Well, that's it. Now ain't that a story for you? The three of them cried and hugged and laughed and cried some more. And Mrs. Carvel didn't die of the shock. It looked like a happy ending, and for her

I reckon it was. She died before Joel had to go to Korea. He got killed. No question or mixup about that. His body was shipped home a week or two after they notified Lafe. It went mighty hard on Lafe. He loved that kid and had big hopes for him.

Lafe's boy went to Vietnam. Ain't that the way with life? It never ends with one story — or one war. Young Lafe was a helicopter pilot. He got home safe and now he has a little boy. Last night I said to Lafe, "Lafe, seems to me like you-all have had a good bit of warring for peaceable folks. I sure hope Sonny don't ever have to go to war."

Lafe, he looks at the coals popping in the grate. Sonny is his eyeballs. I can tell by his face that he's thought a lot about this himself. "Oh . . ." he said, low, like he was going to tell me something serious. But he just smiled that old smile. We might of been fourteen and treading water over in Hanley's. He gave the Old Crow a little shove my way. "Here, old buddy. Sweeten her up a little."

Doll

The place you should spend whatever extra time you have, Wilkie told herself as she neared Middleton, is to stop off and pay Doll a visit. She hadn't been to Middleton but once or twice since Doll had gone to the home, so she hadn't seen her for eight or nine years. Staring through the heavy rain, Wilkie thought of Eugene and smiled. Eugene would have called this a frog-strangler. Doll would have called the heavy thunder a Wagnerian roar.

Doll had been Wilkie's piano teacher and her mother's best friend. The two families faced each other across the street for many years, and for twelve years Doll doggedly dealt with what she described as Wilkie's talent.

"Of course you're gifted," she insisted impatiently, as impatiently as Doll could speak with her soft, low-pitched voice. "All you McIvers are gifted at something. If you're not going to be a painter or a writer, then we've got to make a musician out of you."

Wilkie couldn't have been less interested. When she looked back over all those years of trudging home from school and dragging across the street, music in hand, to Doll's parlor for lessons once a week, she had mixed feelings. "Look both ways," her mother would invariably say—till Wilkie was seventeen years old and struggling with "Country Gardens" for her senior recital.

By the time she stopped for the Biloxi Avenue traffic light, she was laughing. Her musicianship! To this day she would not touch a key in anybody's presence; when she did play, she went in alone in her house, turned back the lid, and faltered through "Humoresque," Handel's "Largo." "Flow Gently, Sweet Afton," maybe.

But how Doll did love music, and she would sit down and play for anybody who asked her. Doll's real name was Alma, but her husband, Eugene Bennett, who ran the cotton compress like his daddy before him, nicknamed her Doll because, he said, "She is my Doll."

When Wilkie was twelve or so and began to sneak the novels of de Maupassant and Flaubert back to her bed to read at night, she commenced to look around for some identifiable *lovers*. Rather surprised, she found herself speculating over Doll and Eugene. They were married, as married as married could be. Nevertheless, Wilkie had determined in her own mind that they were lovers. She strongly suspected they were the only ones in town. Even after she felt pretty sure that they were lovers, Wilkie could never in her most lip-biting fantasies imagine Doll as Emma or Camille, for instance.

But Doll was pretty and vain. She had been middle aged when Wilkie began taking lessons from her. Actually, *Doll* was an inaccurate sobriquet, with its connotations of round rouge spots and embroidered eyelashes like those on the long-legged vamp doll on her guest-room bed. Doll was small and slender, with dark wavy hair, large eyes like black coffee, and a thin, eternally carmine mouth. It was after Wilkie married that she knew to stop saying *Miss Doll*.

"Call me Doll. It makes me feel young," Doll agreed.

Doll composed music and won prizes—published pieces with titles like "Wings on a Spring Night" and "Over a Green Vale" and "Hark! The Mauve Dove."

She was the Methodist church organist, and the Methodist consensus was that the Baptist and Presbyterian organists couldn't hold a candle to Doll Bennett. She listed port and starboard, reaching for those white stops and long wood pedals, always dressed to the nines for church services, weddings, or funerals, where she could move the whole congregation to tears or ecstasy with "The Old Rugged Cross," a Bach fugue, "Träumerei," the wedding marches— a seemingly endless repertoire. She had a little horizontal mirror tilted on the paneled wall above her so she could watch the center aisle, the back of the preacher's head, the spray on the casket, the bride's face, or a baptized baby, and she was expert on timing. Wilkie used to like to stare at Doll's eyes up there in the mirror to see what she was looking at—the big banks of keys, the white stop knobs, the music, the aisle. She was busy.

Doll could really come down on loud chords of heavy music that made the old church vibrate, but she also liked to play soft romantic airs like "Clair de Lune" and "Moonlight Sonata." Wilkie's mother "loved 'The Meditation,' " and her father would ask Doll to play it. "Mr. Edward, I just played that Sunday before last, but I'll play it again before long. How about 'In the Garden' for the offertory next Sunday?" That and "The Old Rugged Cross" were his favorite hymns. Doll played them both at his funeral. That was one of the things she could wade through, playing the favorite music when her oldest and best friends died. No matter how sad she may have felt, she would slide onto the long smooth bench and start reaching right and left for the stops, like she was gathering in all her musical resources appropriate to the departed, who was lying crosswise at the end of the middle aisle.

Doll didn't just love her own musicmaking. She visited the other churches, and she and Eugene traveled to Jackson and New Orleans for concerts and important recitals. They went to Jackson with Wilkie's parents long before Wilkie was born to hear Mary Garden sing *Thaïs*. That was when her mother "fell in love with 'The Meditation,' " and she kept her opera program in her scrapbook for as long as she lived.

When Doll played the piano at home she sometimes closed her eyes and swayed a little. It seemed a little arty to Wilkie, but she was intrigued by it, too. Doll looked dramatic and professional, too enchanted and competent to be interested in how she looked to anybody else.

So she swayed, her hands dangling gracefully during pauses, relaxed over the keys—a technique she tried to teach Wilkie, and in fact succeeded at. She taught Wilkie to approach the piano, to announce her title clearly, to sit down (skirt in place) and slide to the middle of the bench, to poise her foot above the loud pedal, to sit up straight but at ease, take a deliberate deep breath, and raise her hands limp-wristed over the middle octave. All set. She taught Wilkie to rise from the bench with a fair amount of grace and (with a small, grateful smile to the audience) make a relieved getaway. It was that business in between that Wilkie knew she had never really mastered. The most incredible thing she felt she did for Doll was to memorize every piece, no matter how artless the execution. Doll Bennett's pupils did not carry their music to the piano at recitals.

At lessons Doll sat on the bench beside her pupils and watched the interpretation of every phrase. She leaned forward to turn the pages, stirring the air with a faint scent of some cologne Eugene had bought her at the drugstore, helping to recapture rhythm gone astray by conducting a measure or two with both hands, humming or la-la-ing the melody, if there was one.

Wilkie's interest did pick up temporarily when she got a new piece. She would look it over, nervously counting the sharps or flats, calming down if there were no more than three. She would sit in a chair while Doll played it through, usually something Wilkie had heard older girls play at earlier recitals, or, alas, sometimes younger girls. Doll would always remove her rings and drop them into a tiny cutglass bowl that sat on the treble end of the keyboard. Her engagement ring had one of those World War I–type filigree mountings with one diamond, and the wedding ring was a circle of little diamonds. Just like the ones worn by most of the ladies Wilkie studied as she trailed about the town with her mother. Wilkie had never seen Doll play without taking her rings off, and she never saw her get up from the piano without first removing her pince-nez from her small, slightly hooked nose.

Doll was vain. She didn't want to look old, and glasses meant old. But she didn't try to dress like a girl. She loved clothes, and she added exquisite and very feminine new dresses and accessories to her wardrobe with the turns of the seasons.

She would drive seven miles up the brick highway to Middleton to Weill Sisters. Weill Sisters had dresses and hats as stylish as anything you could buy at Kreeger's or Gus Mayer in New Orleans or Kennington's in Jackson. Doll would park her car and walk to Weill Sisters' display windows and stand for a while, forefinger against her upper lip, studying the prints and solids hanging on pale, emaciated manikins. Eventually she would go in and spend an hour or two with one of the old Weill sisters, who were always crimped and painted up, fussing over her, pulling soft sheers, challis, georgettes, handkerchief linens over her head, buttoning, snapping, hooking, plucking, patting, and making a concentrated hard/soft sell to one of their steadiest customers. Finally Doll would come out with a large white dress box, *Weill Sisters* emblazoned on its top in swirling green script. She would lay it on the back seat and drive back down the brick road full of trepidation, doubt, and real fear that she'd bought something inappropriate—too bold in color, cut wrong, too plain or too fancy, or (worst of all) something Eugene wouldn't be enthusiastic about.

Once home, she would spread her purchases out on the bed in the guest room, where there was a long mirror, and telephone Wilkie's mother, who would put down whatever she was doing and say, "I'll be right back. Doll has been up to Weill Sisters." Wilkie tagged along often enough to memorize the scene. She had even accompanied Doll to Weill Sisters. But Doll's shopping bored Wilkie, and she could never reconcile Doll the doll with Doll the musician.

Wilkie suspected that Doll never kept the first article she brought home. She took things back and settled on something else—something that Eugene would insist was just right for her. Sometimes she made a third trip and got the thing she'd first taken back.

Eugene was a big, gentle man, slightly stooped, who whistled a private tune of four or five notes that zig-zagged on the scale. The monotony of that tune seemed to do him no end of good, and its sound at about 5:30 every afternoon signaled Doll to step to the nearest mirror and pat her hair or rub a moistened finger along her dark eyebrows.

Eugene liked to sing. He had a fine bass voice, and he would sit on the piano bench beside Doll and sing hymns and familiar tunes. He liked to sit on their front porch swing and watch the town go by, swinging his legs out, his size fourteen shoes (the largest in town) gleaming.

He never discarded a *Life* magazine or a *National Geographic*. He kept the back numbers stacked in precise order along a wall of the sleeping porch. Wilkie liked to go back to the first number of *Life* or to an ancient *Geographic*. Eugene would say, "Help yourself, but put 'em back in order."

They drove off every summer for a two-week vacation "seeing this great country." Eugene liked to drive to the far west, and the summer their Hupmobile was new they visited the Painted Desert. They brought home a little glass dome filled with sand, many pastel shades of pink and lavender layered to look like mountain peaks and valleys. It sat on their coffee table in the parlor, and Wilkie used to pick it up and study the mountains, which had a distant look to them. The sand was tightly packed and never dislodged to distort the majestic view. Gray felt covered the bottom of the souvenir.

On days when Wilkie was the last piano pupil, or the only one, she and Doll would have a tea party after the lesson. In winter they would sit before the grate, little sparks spewing among the red coals. Doll had a bisque shoe on the mantel, all covered with garlands of pastel flowers. It might have been kicked off by a heedless Watteau courtier. Doll and Wilkie drank hot tea from paper-thin white cups that had a Japanese woman's face embossed in the translucent bottoms; when you turned the cup up for the last swallow there was that glowing, inscrutable, fascinatingly coiffed slant-eyed beauty. Doll would say, "Madame Butterfly," and smile at Wilkie over the teacup.

In summer they took tall glasses of iced tea, flagged with sprigs of mint and wheels of lemon, out on the high back steps off the kitchen—to rattle the ice and drink and, finally, to eat the lemon slice, peel and all. They talked. Wilkie remembered Doll telling more than once how her father had gone with her on the train to enroll her in Goucher College at Baltimore when she was seventeen. He was afraid for her to travel alone. As a railroad attorney, he rode on a pass, and for all the time she was at Goucher he rode the train to take her and bring her back. Before she graduated she eloped with Eugene, with the help of two young married friends.

Her father, a pious man, lived to be nearly a hundred, and Wilkie had thought his little face catlike. She used to look at him and think how a few long stiff hairs on either side of his mouth and a set of small triangular ears would make him an ideal mouser. He apparently grew to accept his son-in-law, for he lived his last twenty-five years peaceably with Eugene and Doll.

Wilkie sat in her car, waiting for the rain to slacken. It came down in sheets, drumming over her head and sheering off the windshield. She turned the engine back on so she could run the wipers at high speed and look out. She could see the Holden County Extended Care Center veiled in water. She began to wonder about Doll inside the building—whether she had a piano in the dayroom, in the room where the old folks congregated to crochet or weave baskets. She realized she had never been in an old people's home—a nursing home. She wondered if Doll might be able to play a Christmas carol or two . . . in her late eighties . . . Could Doll be ninety? If only this rain and lightning would stop.

Doll put on a cantata every Christmas—"The Messiah" more than a few times. The nerve of that little woman—twenty-five voices at the most, many of them borrowed from the Presbyterians, whose pristine little white church faced the Methodists' barnlike old building with its richly bastard architecture, flat stained-glass panes of tantalizing colors, soaring dark beams, warm brass Byzantine-looking chandeliers, frosted lamps aglow. Of course, Doll's pipe organ was superior.

Wilkie used to count those big golden whistles arrayed up and down the wall that curved behind the choir, where her mother sat watching her like a hawk, giving her what Wilkie privately called *Mama's Dracula eye* if her attention strayed from the preacher. However, Wilkie knew that the stained-glass colors reflected on her glasses, so her mother couldn't tell for sure what she was looking at. She laughed aloud. *Mama's Dracula eye . . .*

Wilkie had become so absorbed that for a moment she failed to notice that the rain had slowed to a sprinkle. She quickly stepped out of the car and opened her umbrella. The wind whipped her wetly, blowing her hair over her face and almost taking away her *parasol,* as Doll would say.

The Holden Center was a handsome building, Greek Revival, formerly a lumber baron's home. Added wings stretched out on either side. The interior was spotless. A Christmas tree sparkled, reflected in the leaded panes around the door. Wilkie felt cheered. An attractive receptionist smiled and said yes indeed, she could see Mrs. Bennett. "Go into the back lobby and turn left down the south wing; her room is 304 on your right, about halfway down."

Furling her umbrella, Wilkie stepped through the swinging doors. Wheelchairs sat at random along the walls. There were old ladies, their heads to one side, mouths open, eyes dull or closed, hands idle or fidgeting aimlessly. Wilkie thought of smiling at them, but none of them looked at her. She gave a quick glance around and hurried to the left and down a wide hall toward 304. The beds in most of the rooms were neatly made up. This was a well-kept building. 304 was empty.

"You looking for Miss Doll?" a friendly voice.

"Yes," said Wilkie. "May I see her for a few minutes?"

"Sure. She's back in the TV room. Just go right on back." She pointed to a large open door at the end of the hall.

At the door Wilkie's eyes swept a half-circle of eight or ten wheelchairs, all facing a TV screen. Old, old, old, all asleep. But where was Doll?

"Who you lookin' for, honey?" Another nurse, sweet face, white uniform.

"I was told I'd find Mrs. Bennett back here, but she must be . . . Mrs. Eugene Bennett from Sweet Bay?"

"There she is."

Wilkie looked at faces, the half-wheel of crumpled grotesques. "Where?"

"Right there. Right next to you. Where you from? You kin to Miss Doll?"

Wilkie looked down at the figure close to her left hand, her hand that clutched the parasol. The first image that darted at her was of an old candle stub burned down to a glob, aslant, wax stopped in driplets. Doll's lower lip hung open to one side. Her features seemed to have boiled up larger, looser, and run together; the nose no longer that slightly haughty, pretty little hook. She was sound asleep. Her silk robe was wrapped and tied securely over her undefinable body. Wilkie thought of Weill Sisters.

"*Miss Doll!*" shouted the nurse. Wilkie jumped, startled. "*Miss Doll! Wake up! You got a visitor! Wake up!*" Doll didn't stir. *My God.* Doll was deaf. Wilkie thought of Chopin, Grieg, Sweet Bay.

"Don't disturb her," Wilkie said fearfully. "Don't wake up the others."

"Don't you worry," the nurse smiled. "I'm Dorothy, Miss Doll's sitter." She had a soft smooth tone of voice, when she wasn't shouting. "They all deaf as posts. You ain't gonna bother nobody here. *Miss Doll!*" she yelled. "Who are you?" she asked Wilkie.

"I'm Wilkie McIver. I grew up across the street from her . . . I send her cards . . ."

"Oh yeah, oh yeah. You the one that writes books. I declare! She talk about you." She began to shake Doll. Doll still didn't open her eyes. Finally Wilkie put her mouth near Doll's ear and called out, self-consciously, "*Doll! It's me! Wilkie! Wilkie McIver!*" Doll stirred and opened one eye. The other seemed stuck at first; then it too opened—eyes still dark as coffee but with cream curdling now. She looked dully at nothing.

"You got to yell," said Dorothy. "Go ahead. Holler. You ain't gonna bother those." She passed her hand toward the others, who were still unmoved by the noise or by the soap opera progressing in soundless color on the twenty-five-inch screen.

"Well, does she know people?" Wilkie faltered. What was the use of all this? She had been there less than five minutes, and it seemed like an hour. "I don't want to . . ."

Dorothy leaned over and shook Doll's shoulder again. "*Miss Doll!*" she bellowed. Doll raised her head slowly and her milky eyes began to turn toward Wilkie's face, which was squarely in front of her as Wilkie half-knelt before her wheelchair.

"*Wilkie?*" Doll shouted and reached for Wilkie's hands. Intelligence collected in her eyes. "*Wilkie!*" she shouted again.

"*Doll!*" Wilkie yelled. "*I'm in town for an hour or so, and I wanted to say hello!*"

"*What?*" Her voice was big and hoarse from shouting. It sounded like somebody else's.

Dorothy shouted, "*She here for a minute and want to see you.*"

Doll gestured with her hand. "Come on," said Dorothy, "Miss Doll want to go in her room to visit."

Walking back to 304 Wilkie worried about trying to communicate and wondered why Doll didn't wear a hearing aid. How could they talk? She was obviously tranquilized—they all were. This was a house of sleep; Wilkie could see that. She asked Dorothy, "Does she really know me? Can we . . . talk?"

"Sure," said Dorothy. "She bright as a dollar in her mind. She don't forget nothing. She deaf and can't see much—sees color, not much more—but her mind, it good as ever." She wheeled Doll around, spokes glinting, beside the bed, and Wilkie sat on a small chair close beside her. Dorothy took up a hairbrush and began smoothing Doll's hair. There wasn't a white hair visible. But Doll didn't have on makeup. Wilkie thought, *Doll didn't deserve this. Geriatrics be damned.*

Wilkie took a copy of her new book from her bag and wrote in it, "For Doll, who never gave up on me. With love, Wilkie," and laid it in her lap. Doll picked it up and held it out in front of her, trying, but failing, to read the title.

"*Did you write this?*" she shouted.

"*Yes,*" Wilkie shouted back.

"*What's it called?*"

"*This Is Living.*"

"*What?*" she shouted, frowning.

"*This Is Living.*" Wilkie screamed at Doll.

"Oh." Her voice dropped, still hoarse, but with a certain reminder of Doll's tone. She could see Wilkie had written something on the half-title page, for she handed the book to Dorothy.

"*What's it say? Read what Wilkie wrote.*" Doll hollered.

Dorothy got down close to Doll's ear and shouted, "*To Doll, who never gave up on me. Love, Wilkie.*"

Doll's eyes looked at Wilkie's, and tears rose to the rims. She looked down at her arthritic, ringless hands. She raised a hand toward a cluttered dresser. Wilkie saw the bisque Watteau shoe and the domed painted desert, a picture of a youthful Eugene, smiling, hair parted in the middle. And a set of earphones.

"Her nephew, you know, Mr. what's-his-name down at Sweet Bay, Mr. George," said Dorothy. "He come up on Wednesdays and Sundays and bring records of music for her to listen to. She tell him what she want to hear, and he get it. Clamps them things over her ears, and I turn it up high. She just love it, I tell you. She live for it." Dorothy sang the word *lee-uv,* drawing it out in emphasis.

"Can she really hear it? Enjoy it?"

"Sure. She say she hear it fine, just love it. Nods her head, keeping time. Wave her hands." Dorothy smiled.

"George is bringing 'The Goldberg Variations' Wednesday, Landowski," shouted Doll. *"Chopin and Grieg last week."*

Wilkie stood up. She had no time left.

"I'm coming back to see you," she shouted in Doll's ear. While Doll held her hands, Wilkie kissed her forehead. She had never kissed Doll before.

As she walked down the hall she heard Doll bellow hoarsely to Dorothy. *"I remember the afternoon she was born. She was the baby of the family. All those McIvers were gifted."*

Joanna

So even the Lattimore children have to die.
There was a time when we thought we were all immortal.
                                        from "Isabel"
                                        by Richard Lattimore

A few great raindrops began to smack the dusty windshield. Virginia
pressed her finger against the chrome button, but the windshield
washer was empty, and the blades of the wiper groaned against the
dry glass. She slowed down and squinted, trying to see through the
brown arcs. *Oh, for a good shower.*
                    Dr. Foster went to Gloster
                    In a shower of rain.
                    Stepped in a puddle
                    Up to his middle
                    And never went there again.
    She looked in the rearview mirror to see what she looked like, recit-
ing childhood verse on her way to her sister's funeral. Dr. Foster
was part of a shift into the past that began yesterday, almost the
moment her brother called. As they talked, it was as though someone
kept switching television channels from the evening news to an old
movie.
    "I have some sad news for you, Virginia. Joanna was found dead
this morning," her brother began.
    "What? Joanna? How . . ."
    Then she was only half-hearing Richard. Her eyes were fixed on
the folds of a rust-colored dish towel that lay at the edge of the sink,
but she was seeing Joanna at sixteen, dressing herself up in old clothes
in Mama's big linen closet, pushing her red hair under an old felt

hat of Daddy's, turning herself into a hobo. Virginia had watched the transformation in wonderment. Ten years younger than Joanna, she believed Joanna could do anything. Everybody in town talked about her talents, her gleaming hair, her green eyes, green as winter rye, they said. She was always acting in plays, singing, dancing, playing the piano, painting. She carved Mozart's head out of a bar of Ivory soap and set it beside the metronome.

But that day Joanna had slipped out of the house and around to the back door and knocked loudly. It was 1934 and tramps knocked often, poorly dressed jobless men begging to earn a meal—rake some leaves, clean out the gutters, chop some wood.

Mama walked to the door, Virginia right behind her, trying not to giggle. Mama didn't recognize Joanna and told the tramp she'd warm him a plate of greens and cornbread left from dinner that he could eat on the back steps. Mama never turned anyone away, but if Daddy wasn't home she wouldn't let a stranger come inside. No white God-fearing southern lady would. When Mama turned to go into the kitchen Joanna, still disguising her voice, came boldly into the house. Mama screamed and grabbed Virginia, sure that after all her years of warnings she and one of her four daughters were about to be "assaulted." Racing up the hall into the library, she slammed the door and jammed it with a spindly chair, all the time screaming hysterically. Beside her, Virginia was trying to be heard: "Mama, Mama, it's only Joanna!" And outside the door Joanna was about to die laughing and was shouting, rattling the knob against a carved rose on the chair's back. "Mama, it's just me. It's me, Mama."

Finally, Mama heard both her daughters, and her fear changed to outrage. Incredulous, she opened the door and slapped Joanna in the face, hard. She never forgave Joanna. Never could she laugh about it. It became a symbol of Joanna's wrongheadedness, just as her red hair, like Daddy's, symbolized a hot temper. Joanna was a *McCall, not a Leger*. It was true.

So when Brother paused Virginia had to force herself to understand what he had said. Joanna had been lying dead on her kitchen floor, knocked on her back by a massive coronary, a bag of groceries spilled around her. She had been dead four days. There would be graveside services—tomorrow, Sunday afternoon, at four.

"V.A.? Are you OK?"

"Yes. Yes. Of course. I'm just . . . so sorry. I'll be there. I'll meet you at Nelda's, after noon." Now she was seeing Joanna lying there like a doll, arms and legs spread out, the red hair now white, the fingernails that she once laughingly put bright green polish on now white. "I'll be there."

Hanging up, she turned to her husband. "Joanna's dead. Brother went to see why she didn't answer the phone. Found her on the kitchen floor. A massive coronary, he said."

Stephen's face sagged. "Oh. I'm sorry, Virginia. I'm sorry."

Virginia looked away. She knew his chin was trembling. He did that since his stroke. It had been called a light stroke, but now even a sentimental TV commercial caused his eyes to well up, and he would have to swallow if he tried to talk. Stephen had been fond of Joanna when she was young and gorgeous and full of fun and ideas. Everybody had. But he hadn't seen her in years, ten maybe. Neither of them had.

Joanna didn't like Virginia. Virginia had learned to live with the fact. It had been more than a decade since she'd lain awake nights on end, thinking about what had happened to Joanna to make her hostile to her whole family, not only Virginia. And when Virginia quit trying so hard to understand, acceptance came. Accepting meant leaving Joanna alone. That was all Joanna seemed to want, finally. Privacy. And bourbon. Virginia, living in New Orleans, could stay away.

Joanna married Kip Rankin when she was eighteen, virtually skipping the porch-swing segment of her social development. When Mama and Daddy had found out that she was serious about Kip, a good-natured senior at Ole Miss who played saxophone and rode his huge roan horse right up to the gallery and pulled Joanna up behind his western saddle, they had thrown up their hands.

The pretense of cheer faltered early at the wedding. Miss Winnie Rankin broke into audible weeping and was comforted by, of all people, Mama, who startled even eight-year-old Virginia by saying, "Miss Winnie, look at it like I do. I'm not losing a daughter, I'm gaining a son." This precipitated a still noisier outcry from Miss Winnie, who was full of proverbs. "Your daughter's your daughter all her life. Your son's your son till he gets him a wife," she said. As Joanna cut the cake she said, "There's no fool like an old fool." Virginia figured she meant Miss Winnie, who looked old. Daddy walked out on the gallery and stared out across the lawn, where Mama had set up tables for lunch.

When Joanna's freewheeling ebullience persisted after she was "adult" and married to Kip, who went next door to kiss his mother goodnight every night until she died just before he did, old heads nodded over Joanna and watched impatiently for her to settle down to behavior prescribed for young wives in Sweet Bay. But she continued, as a married woman, to wear short shorts and bounce with the rhythm of her baby grand as she beat out jazz and swing. She chain smoked, learned to drink bourbon with Kip and his friends, and developed a laugh you could hear a block away. She was just too much, they sighed. She was also as sensitive as a fresh wound. Nobody ever seemed to catch onto that. If the gypsies who used to camp every spring out in the Heaslips' pasture had stolen Joanna, what a life she could have lived.

Joanna's laughter lost its mirth. At thirty she was an alcoholic, by forty an eccentric recluse, and at fifty a widow. She would have been sixty had she lived another month. For years she had been one of the town's many drunks. She had locked her doors, literally, against her family, sometimes even her own grown sons. She locked Mama out — Mama now long dead of her own heart attack. She locked Daddy out, who lived twenty years a widower, but not before she made off with some of his favorite possessions — furniture, odds and ends. He had disinherited her before he put out his last Pall Mall and hacked his final emphysemic cough. He spent his last decade in bitterness, glad to be steadfastly furious enough with this child to "cut her out — a disgrace to us all." As he railed against Joanna he never evoked one recognizable image of her. She had become a monster, foreign, his fascinating, redheaded McCall child.

Well, now she was dead. Virginia walked around Stephen, to the french doors, and stared out across the patio to the water dripping off a piece of slate into the fish pool, making rings that bumped into lily pads. Boomer, the Australian shepherd, trotted up to the door, something in his mouth.

"Stephen! Boomer's got a rat in his mouth. Oh, my God." A black leg and a long hairless tail hung out of the big dog's mouth. "Oh, God." She ran to the bathroom and slammed the door. When she came out, Boomer had disappeared. Now she began to fear that the rat might have been poisoned, and she dialed the vet. No answer. After awhile Boomer came back onto the patio, apparently in good health, his great eyes, as always, disconcertingly humble, no evidence of the wretched sight. Virginia was fond of the dog, but now she could not bear to get near him.

A call came from her sister in Asheville, who had just received her call from Brother. Marjorie was weeping. "I'm so far away. Oh, poor Joanna. Oh, I know. I know. We couldn't help her. We all tried. Oh, how poor Mother tried. Virginia! Four days! Do you realize . . . ? Virginia, honey, please explain to everyone why I'm not there. Tell May Ella and F.O. and Helen Sanders, all of them, tell them that I simply cannot make the trip. I'm no longer young. Even if I'd been able to go, I've been caught without a decent black dress — for a funeral in the family, I mean. Explain . . . I'll probably die way up here and nobody will find me. No. That will never happen to me. I have too many friends. I wonder if Nelda will rise from her couch and attend her own sister's funeral. I'll bet she won't. She'll have some excuse — and right there only ten miles away." Nelda was the eldest sister.

"Probably not. I'm going directly to her house. If she and Frank can go, we'll all go together. Don't worry about that. And I'll speak to people for you. But remember, I haven't been up there for years. I might not know them. They might not know me." After she hung up, she and Stephen decided that she should drive up to Mississippi alone.

Virginia went about her business all that day. They were having yard work done, and she and Stephen were in and out of the house supervising the man who was putting in a new border of liriope, moving crape myrtles along the driveway, trimming the fig vine — all established from cuttings and roots from Mama and Daddy's place. She sat down on the brick wall by the fish pool, watching the fantails of the goldfish waving like gossamer on a soft breeze, and thought of Daddy's fish pool under the big magnolia in the front-yard. His fish were enormous and his lilies and hyacinths fragrant. He had covered the pool with chickenwire. It was shallow, but Mama frequently reminded him of the Cables' child who "drowned at two years while playing in a galvanized washtub in the backyard. It only takes a teacupful." She usually added a word about the dangers of blisters on the heel, President Coolidge's son having died from an infected blister after a game of tennis. Both of these sad events belonged to history long past, but they were sufficiently horrifying examples of carelessness for Mama, who went to extremes to shield her children.

Joanna had malaria during the summer that she was fifteen. A cousin who was going away to college gave her four big scrapbooks of movie stars — pasted pictures of thin women with narrow arched eyebrows, dressed in long satin gowns edged with great rolls of white fur. The men leaned on polo mallets or gold-headed walking canes. Joanna adored the books and she collected more pictures and more books. She pasted her pictures with flour paste that she stirred up in a teacup. Sometimes she would leave the cup on her windowsill until the paste soured and gray mold formed on it. She forbade Virginia ever to take the scrapbooks out of the window seat in her room. Virginia did sneak in and raise the lid and open the top book to study the sepia faces — Billie Dove, Francis X. Bushman, Mary Pickford, Douglas Fairbanks, Vilma Banky. But she never looked for long, fearing that Joanna would catch her. Maybe Joanna would have liked her better if she'd found out and they could have had a big fight and become friends.

Joanna never had another childhood illness that Virginia could remember, but she *cheated Death* one afternoon out in Buckley's pasture. A barnstorming pilot was taking passengers up for rides in his little Waco, and Daddy took Joanna to the pasture and paid two dollars for her to have a thrilling ten-minute ride. When the two of them came home, with Joanna's red hair blown six ways to Sunday, Mama accused Daddy of risking one of his children's lives. Joanna, she said, had simply *cheated Death*. They were two of a kind, McCalls through and through. Daddy called Mama *an anachronism* and returned to his office in a huff. But Joanna didn't seem to mind. Virginia asked her what it was like, and Joanna said,

"Do you mean flying? Or cheating Death?" Virginia had thought they were one and the same.

Soon after Virginia crossed the state line she began to see the green Mississippi hills rolling off before her, a pleasant sight after the unrelieved flatlands of south Louisiana. On toward Jackson the interstate lay like white straps binding the hills ahead too tightly, slicing through red clay that reminded Virginia of raw beef. How could the trees be so green in a drought? She looked for a pond or a creek — water was her metaphor. Without it she could hardly express herself.

At Pontchatoula she drove off the exit and into a service station where an attendant hosed off her windshield and polished it with brown paper towels. Virginia thanked the man.

Back on the interstate she drove on northward, past her hometown, where her dead sister's house now sat empty, and past the used car lot where the old family home had been — a big house that for decades had bulged to its wraparound galleries with the explosive clutch of siblings who were more confusion than comfort to their parents. And past Brother's, where he now monitored his poor health with his third wife in his in-laws' old home, high-backed rockers lined up on the porch, surely still slipcovered in tan Indianhead piped in green. The interstate took her around it all.

On to the next town, and Nelda's house with Nelda's French bedroom upstairs, and Frank's gold coin collection in a safe "on the premises," according to family legend. Nelda and Frank had recently returned from a business trip to Switzerland.

Frank didn't hear Virginia's ring at the iron-grilled door from the terrace, so she let herself into the back sitting room. A black man sat on a straight chair near the door. He looked toward her, expressionless. But Frank sprang to his feet, apologizing. He'd been watching a football game from a dark blue leather sofa. Two identical sofas faced each other across the big room — his and hers. "Virginia, I didn't expect you this soon." He seemed unaware of the man in the chair. She looked back at the man who ignored her and stared at the TV.

"I thought I'd better come on if we're to go by the funeral home. Is Nelda . . .?"

"Nelda isn't going. She's feeling bad. There is no — ah — calling at the funeral home, only the graveside service. You and I will go to the cemetery and meet Joanna's boys and their families. They all got in last night. They're sleeping at the Holiday Inn. They couldn't stay at . . . I'd have had them all come here, but you know how it is with Nelda not feeling well. Richard took to his bed after he called you and Marjorie. I think all this just got him down too much, and his blood pressure ran up. He and Joanna . . . You know . . . He called a while ago." Frank's fragments seemed appropriate.

"I see."

Virginia's thoughts went back to Joanna's sons, men with children of their own. Joanna had been a devoted and loving mother to them when they were small. She told them wonderful tales at bedtime—fantastic serials that went on night after night. The boys had adored her. Which was worse, Virginia wondered, a loving drunken mother or a shrewish drunken mother? You could just hate a shrew. But a laughing, rollicking den mother stumbling about among the Cub Scouts serving fantastic brownies . . .

Did Joanna ever write her children's stories down? She painted in oils almost until the time of her death. Virginia knew that. And when Joanna was a young teenager she ordered boxes of printed Christmas cards and handpainted them in watercolor. Ringing doorbells up and down the street, she sold all her boxes in an afternoon and made eighteen dollars. A child capable of earning eighteen dollars during the Depression was not ordinary. Virginia could see Joanna now, setting up the card table in front of the fireplace in her room and arranging the paints, a Ball jar of water, and the dull little cards that Joanna brought to life as she filled in the red on holly berries and Santa suits and green on holly leaves and Christmas trees.

While Frank took Virginia's handbag, a black woman came downstairs and left with the man. Frank said to them, "Thank y'all for coming." He walked into the kitchen and announced Virginia's presence on the intercom. Nelda's familiar, young-sounding voice came back: "Oh, is she already here? Tell her to give me a few minutes."

Virginia sat down in a Chinese Chippendale chair that didn't hit her back right.

"Drink? How about a martini—want vodka and tonic? It's so hot outside." He smiled his peculiar smile. He had a tic in his right cheek that Virginia had noticed since she was a child.

"No, nothing, thanks." Virginia was thinking that Nelda would look her over and find her still strangely careless of fashion. That had once depressed her. She smiled. Soon she was summoned upstairs. Nelda was propped up in her French hand-decorated bed, frothy white eyelet-edged sheet and pillowcases framing her frail person. She wore aqua satin pajamas and robe. Her white face and short hairstyle were all the whiter for her large dark-rimmed spectacles. Diamonds shot red and blue and gold from her ears and hands and the pendant on her chest. Stephen couldn't abide Nelda. "Prima donna," he'd said, and "They're all prima donnas." Meaning her whole family. That had depressed her, too.

She walked to the bedside and kissed Nelda's very soft cheek. Nelda had no visible eyebrows. She spoke words of welcome, adding, "You haven't been here in three years." Virginia wondered if she was accusing her of neglect. Her last visit about a year before had been an obvious intrusion.

"Francis is much more upset over this than I am. It came as no surprise to me. I've been expecting it for years. Joanna withdrew from family and all society years ago. I knew that sooner or later this very thing would happen. Now it has. The last time she came here—two or three years ago—she went straight to the bar—it was ten o'clock in the morning—and she revisited it several times before she left—about noon. She didn't seem intoxicated. I've been interviewing a woman—a maid."

"Oh. Are you going to hire her?"

"I am not."

"Oh?"

"When they walk in here like that—I've been through all this too often—they're all ruined. The Roosevelts started it. You can't remember all that."

"Nor the defeat of the Armada. Nor Appomattox."

"What?"

"Has Hattie quit?"

"No, but she can't be here every hour of every day. I've got to have somebody to fill in, Virginia. I'm an invalid. I seldom go downstairs. Nobody realizes how bad my health is. Those ridiculous doctors in Houston and New Orleans, all the rest, they refuse to listen to me. What are those tests? Nothing. Absolutely nothing. Francis traipses from clinic to clinic with me, but he doesn't know how bad I feel—or care."

Frank entered with a large silver tray and put it on the coffee table before the oyster white moiré sofa where Virginia sat. On the tray were two Madeira tea napkins, pimento-cheese sandwiches on Spode plates, and two silver tumblers filled with ice and Coke. He smiled and murmured something and went back downstairs. Soon he returned with a plate and set it on a white wicker bedtray for Nelda. Virginia tried to imagine him slapping Nelda's face. Marjorie claimed she saw him do it one night in Antoine's. Virginia looked at him and said, "Frank?"

"Hmmm?"

"Did you make this pimento cheese? It's great." She wondered how he'd have looked if she'd said, "You remind me of a maitre d'."

"I made it. Yeah." He smiled. "But I didn't think it was so good."

"It's delicious. I make it in my Cuisinart. Do you?"

"What is a Cuisinart?" asked Nelda.

"A food processor," said Virginia.

"A what? Oh—I don't know about that. Do we have one, Francis? I'm sure we do, since you can't resist any fad or gadget. I never go in the kitchen—haven't been to a grocery store in ten years."

"Who shops?"

"Hattie. Or Francis."

"Well, it is depressing. You're better out of it," Virginia conceded.

"Yeah," said Frank. "V.A., have I given you my gumbo recipe? Did I ever send you a copy?"

"With the instructions to take a drink between steps? After the roux . . ."

"Yeah—well," he laughed. "I don't make a roux, you know."

"Oh, that's right. I remember now. I'll have to watch you make it sometime. I make a dark roux first, then turn it down and sauté the chopped green stuff in it."

"Yours is probably better. I just use a lot of tomatoes and stir in some thickening."

"Well, I seldom use tomato. I make a really dark bottom-of-the-bayou gumbo—lots of okra—whole baby okra."

"Francis, why don't you go on downstairs so Virginia and I can visit? You can visit with her at the cemetery."

Frank picked up the trays. "I'll go get dressed, and maybe I can see the rest of the Saints game. They're getting clobbered, as usual."

Nelda talked dispassionately of Joanna. Virginia listened with one ear, as Mama used to say, but she was thinking her own thoughts, scarcely hearing Nelda say that Joanna lay in a plastic bag, unembalmable.

Virginia's thoughts rushed to the rich green Asian groundcover that the man was spreading about the beds in her own yard, and to the squared boxwoods he trimmed with his hand clippers, though she'd offered her electric ones. He spoke only Sicilian, so he demonstrated his contempt for electric shears by breaking off a woody sprig of box and chewing at it with his teeth till it was splayed out like an old paintbrush. He held it out and Virginia got the message, though his twenty-year-old daughter, who worked with him, laughed and translated. Virginia thought of Boomer at the french doors, swallowing the vile rat. Quickly she moved her thoughts on to the azalea bed across the back yard, flowering shrubs now cut free of strangling honeysuckle by the man and his daughter.

When Joanna was eleven she had boarded the Illinois Central's Number 3 one morning and ridden forty miles northward to Claybrook for a visit with Mama's sister and her son, Junius. Mama's descriptions of Joanna's departure in navy pleated skirt, white middy blouse, and thick red braids tied with navy ribbons were so vivid that Virginia fancied she could remember going down to the train station with her. Maybe she had been there. Joanna took with her a *Delineator* magazine in which were pressed many bright tissue linings she had saved from Christmas card envelopes. She arrived safely in Claybrook and was driven to Aunt Virginia's white antebellum Greek Revival far out on Chattahoochie Avenue.

That night she and Junius made trains from shoeboxes strung together. Junius had saved boxes for her visit, and they pasted

Joanna's colored papers over the square windows and fastened candle stubs in the boxes. They pulled their long, glowing train up and down the front walk until Aunt Virginia made them come in. Then they pulled the train up and down the length of a storeroom on the second floor. After the family had gone to bed, fire roared out of the storeroom, and Aunt Virginia, Junius, and Joanna escaped down a sturdy rose trellis. That day Mama and Daddy drove up the gravel highway to Claybrook to fetch Joanna. Whatever traumas resulted were unknown to Virginia. The family seldom talked about the fire. Aunt Virginia's husband, Junius, Sr., who didn't live at home, quickly built a fine ugly red brick house that had lights in the closets and sparkling glass doorknobs.

Nelda got out of bed and showed Virginia four new pairs of pumps she'd ordered from Neiman-Marcus — white, rust, bone, black. They were still in the boxes, each pump wrapped in tissue.

"Hmmm. They're beautiful." They were 5½ AAAAAs.

Nelda's pale blue room had four large closets with double sliding doors. One door was open slightly, revealing three mink coats of different lengths.

"Virginia, Francis is a very rich man. But he's stingy. I get the same allowance I got ten years ago."

"That must be tough. When the cost of food is so inflated."

"Oh, I don't pay for the food."

Virginia went into the dressing room and combed her hair, touched her mouth with lipstick. Nelda's lipstick was scarlet, as always. Her heavy silver dresser things lay in perfect order, with other articles of Waterford, Lenox.

Frank was immaculate in a cream suit when Virginia went downstairs. It was hard to believe that he was nearly seventy. They went to the cemetery in his Mercedes. He drove down the interstate very fast. Virginia wished he would slow down. He was talking animatedly, boyishly, complimenting her on her career — said he was proud of her. She thanked him, surprised.

"Oh, damn," he said. "I've passed the turnoff."

"Just get off at the next exit — the old Maysburg Road — and go back up on the old highway." How easily she remembered.

"OK. That's right. No problem." And he went on chatting as

though he were enjoying her company. He didn't talk about Joanna. Then they were driving up the little curving road to the old cemetery. Virginia was startled. She had not imagined the scene. Cars lined the road on both sides. A large crowd half-circled a green funeral canopy. The Cadillac hearse looked absurd parked nearby. Virginia realized now that Joanna was to be buried across the road in the "new part" next to Kip, and not in the large plot under the holly in the old section where their parents were buried.

For the first time she felt a rush of emotions, too many, too fast to be sorted out. She could only think that she was not thinking clearly. *Joanna, what happened?* Frank parked as close to the canopy as possible. She waited for him to open the door. She was back where men opened doors, invariably. She took his cream elbow and said, "Let's just go sit on the back row of the chairs. I'm afraid I won't be able to remember names . . . It's been so long . . ."

"All right."

She sat down facing the bronze coffin with its blanket of red roses. Red! Red McCall. Joanna had been called that in high school. Mama was horrified, forbade it. She also put her foot down about Jo. And V.A. for Virginia. No nicknames. Virginia looked away, to the west, toward the tall holly that shaded the McCall his and her granite stone, and back, into the face of a man she had grown up with. She stood up quickly and went to meet him, and then many old friends came to her and spoke kindly — very kindly. She recognized girlhood friends of Joanna's, and some of her own. One stout matron, every mahogany-veneered hair in place, embraced her and said, "Virginia, you don't remember me, but I'm Marilyn Best — I was Marilyn Carr. It's been what? Twenty years?"

"Of course. Marilyn." Marilyn had told her there was no Santa Claus one fall afternoon as they played dolls on the back porch.

A paunchy bald man — Jim Ed Rollins. He'd taken her paste brush on their first day at school and the teacher, her first cousin, couldn't "show favoritism" by retrieving Virginia's brush. She'd heard Jim Ed was president of his Dad's bank now, and she had imagined that lower lip coming forward as he held somebody's money in his pudgy hand, above his shoulder, saying, "You can't have this. It's mine." When he took her hand she discovered three of his fingers were missing.

Then Joanna's sons and their wives and children were under the canopy with her. Greetings and embraces were hasty, for one of the two ministers began reading passages from the Bible. "In My Father's house are many mansions. If it were not so, I would have told you . . ." A favorite passage of their mother's. Virginia had never seen either of the ministers. They wore dark suits and vests despite the sweltering heat, and they took turns reading verses from their Bibles. There was no eulogy — not a word about Joanna. Virginia sighed carefully. She felt miserable and sad. She had thought the McCalls were such a family! That she was uniquely lucky to have three grown sisters, tall, vivid, adored. She had to be told after she was grown that Joanna resented her for displacing her as the baby of the family. Sibling rivalry. The cliché had sounded so silly to her. It still did. The red roses were swimming. Everything was.

The heat bore down on the green canopy. The heavy humid air was becoming unbearably oppressive and Virginia could hardly breathe. Her cover of sturdy calm and nostalgia had begun to fall from her like a heavy garment as the heat forced the sickening reality against her. *Four days, Virginia. Four days. Oh, my God, Joanna.* She lowered her head and took shallow breaths of terrible air, flavored faintly with the familiar scents rising from her own breast.

She could not now lift her eyes to the coffin and the red roses, Red McCall's coffin stinking in the hot Mississippi sun on a Sunday afternoon in the new part of the cemetery that had no marble angels, when everyone should be at home singing around the piano under the ceiling fan in the old house. Her hand was stuck to the dark blue leather of her handbag.

One of the ministers was saying *amen*. It was done. She looked at her watch. They had been there fifteen minutes. As they rose from their chairs a sudden rain began to drum on the canvas. The back half of the crowd ran to the parked cars. The front half tried to crowd under the canopy. Some of the people began to hug her and remind her of who they were. "We'd love to have you come by . . ." Then Frank took her arm, and a man from the funeral home sheltered them under his big black umbrella to Frank's car.

Going home, Frank drove through the little town. He drove past the old home place, now lined with a skimpy row of used cars that sat where the back yard had begun. The big live oak with its gnarled playhouse roots that spread to the street's edge was gone, and the magnolia, and the chinaberry by the south porch where she had climbed and sat and dreamed, and the pecans and the figs and crab-apples down at the back. The old Wheeler house next door still stood, humiliated, like a once-beautiful woman painted grotesquely for whoring, signs nailed to its gallery columns, all the sweet bays and magnolias gone. Frank didn't seem to notice where they were. Probably he passed this way often.

"Were many people there?" asked Nelda, when Virginia returned to the ice blue room. "Jessie McPherson?"

"Yes. She was there."

"Corinne Cooper? Helen Sanders?"

"Yes."

She called more names. "What was it like?" She held her cigarette vertically before her eyes, like a pencil.

"It was over quickly," said Virginia.

Driving home, Virginia passed the turnoff to the curving old Catamawa road where, before they were married, she and Stephen used to take Sunday afternoon drives under the moss-hung trees. He would stop occasionally and they would kiss. The road led to a convent where several of her Catholic friends had attended school. She smiled. They had all cursed like sailors, fascinatingly, and they had said they learned how from the nuns. She looked ahead, down the interstate lowering itself out of the gentle hills of Mississippi.

Just a Little Sore Throat

I could tell you any number of things about my Aunt Etta, who was married to my father's older brother. She and Uncle Maury had no children, and I liked to think of myself as their surrogate daughter. Aunt Etta was a fine lady, modest, retiring, a homebody who never craved any special attention. Nevertheless, she had a feature that made her instantly noticeable, one about which she could, in her day, do absolutely nothing. She had an uncommonly large bosom. There was in all the county no match for her and so she bore, ingenuously, a certain notoriety. It was a matter that people could not resist joking about, and regardless of all her good qualities, when her name came up or she walked into a room she became the unwitting star.

Oh, the things I'd heard my friends at school say about her! Sometimes, I confess, I joined in the laughter. They didn't mean any harm when they said things like:

"Mrs. Summerfield hasn't seen her navel in thirty years."

"She can't bend over 'cause she'd never get up again."

"Wonder who trims her toenails. M-M-Maury?"

"She ought to divide those things up among you flatties."

"Ooh, here comes Mrs. Big Tits!"

If it sounds mean or banal, let me just tell you that there wasn't much going on around there, and such things as making jokes about Aunt Etta's bust simply filled a need for entertainment. In Sweet Bay laughing at people was a way of life, often much crueler than any jokes directed at my Aunt Etta. Well, I'll have to say she was enormous — each one about half a bushel. Poor Aunt Etta did carry a load up front, they said. Came down the church aisle "like a dreadnaught."

"Mountainous."

"Colossal."

"Jumbo."

Uncle Maury stuttered a bit, and he couldn't say Aunt Etta's name without putting an *Uh* in front of it. When he spoke to her or of her he said *Uh-Etta.* Everybody knew this and laughed about it, too. Some people never referred to her any way but as Uh-Etta. I don't think she knew this, though she certainly noticed that Uncle Maury always said it. Uncle Maury might have been the least bit intimidated by his noticeable wife. All such speculations aside, they were a happy couple, and I knew them as well as anybody knew them. Both had wonderful senses of humor, though I can't imagine anyone ever testing either with a reference to Aunt Etta's frontage.

One morning when I dropped in on them fairly early, as I often did in the summertime, Uncle Maury met me at the door and said, "Annie, your Aunt Uh-Etta has a sore throat. I'm trying to get her to see the d-doctor. I'm on my way to a meeting in New Orleans, so I can't keep arguing with her."

"Uh-Etta," he pleaded, as we went into the kitchen, "here's Annie. Now she could drive you over to see that new d-doctor. Call him!"

"Sure, I'll be glad to take you, Aunt Etta."

Aunt Etta sat at the kitchen table, her jugs resting there like saddlebags filled with gold. She coughed and the table walked an inch or so on the linoleum.

"Oh, Maury. It's just a little sore throat."

"Uh-Etta, I've got to go. Now, I'm going to depend on you to be sensible. This has gone on long enough. Call that d-doctor, Annie." He leaned over and kissed Aunt Uh-Etta on the top of her gray hair. He tapped me on the shoulder and pointed toward the phone in the hall.

"G-gargle some hot salty water," he called over his shoulder as he shut the kitchen screened door behind him.

Aunt Etta looked at me. "I've been gargling since this first hit me. Hasn't helped a bit." She adjusted the top on the sugar bowl. "Oh shuckins, I guess I'll call him." She picked up the thin phone book. "What's his name, now? Powell? Tower?"

"Power, Auntie. Dr. Henry Power. But he isn't in the phone book yet. I'll call Birdie so you won't have to talk."

I went into the hall and cranked the little oak Western Electric box on the wall.

"Number, please," said Birdie.

"Birdie," I said, "what's the new doctor's number?"

"Who's sick?" asked Birdie, popping her spearmint.

"Nobody's sick. Just Aunt Etta has a sore throat."

"Well, honey, I hope it don't go down into her chest. Miss Uh-Etta would have big trouble if she got a chest cold. Hee hee. 417. I'll connect you. Just hold your horses, hon."

"Thanks, Birdie." Honestly!

The morning sun was coming through the stained-glass door at the back of the hall, and it made pretty glimmers on the pine floor on either side of the old red runner. Aunt Etta stood as close beside me as she could get, trying to hear. She felt soft.

Both of our old doctors had died, and everybody was glad when Dr. Power came to take over. He'd hired Miss Ruby Burris as his office nurse, and Mother said she was wearing her white uniform and cap at all times — looking much more professional than when she'd hired out for home duty all those years. We didn't have a hospital, but the new doctor was supposed to be working on that.

"Miss Ruby, this is Annie Summerfield. Aunt Etta has had a sore throat for three days. Could Doctor Power see her right away?"

"Sore thote, huh?" said Miss Ruby. I could just see her overbite, "Better get her right over here this afternoon. She might have diphtheria. Those Hughes kids out at Mount Ararat all have it. Uh-Etta been exposed to anything?"

"Oh, I don't think so. Aunt Etta . . ."

"You just bring her on over at two o'clock. Only thing is, I won't be here. Got to run up to Middleton and give some shots. But bring her right on in and Doctor will see her. I'll fill out a card for us."

"Oh, my mercy," said Aunt Etta when I hung up. "I hate putting him out for a little old sore throat."

"That's what he's here for, isn't it? Besides, he probably needs the business. I hear he charges five dollars for an office visit and ten for a house call."

"You don't mean it!" gasped Aunt Etta, laying her hand on top of her bosom. "Why, Dr. Butler never charged over two for an office visit, and I think it was four for a house call, any time of day or night. Maury says these young doctors will drive us to socialized medicine, and he may be right." She sank down again. Like the Titanic, the bow went down last.

"Come on, now, Auntie. This is no time to be chintzy. It's your health! I've got to go home, but I'll be back at ten till two and honk for you."

"I'll be ready," said Aunt Etta, hoisting herself back up from a chair. She listed forward slightly as she got her balance. She was good at it, but then she'd been doing it for a long time.

"I had a heavy bust right from the first," she'd once told me. I'll say. Aunt Etta had to reach around her bosom to get to her dinner plate.

When I came back for Aunt Etta she was all bathed and weighting the air with Cashmere Bouquet bath powder. She had her hair carefully caught up behind, very dignified, with twenty or thirty silver-colored hairpins. She was perspiring a little and flapping at her face with her jabot that lay like a fluted napkin on a dinner table. She had on her black patent pumps.

"Gee, Aunt Etta, you sure got dressed up."

"I want to make a good impression." She added, "Oh, Annie, you're sweet to drive me. I'm so glad your mother let you go ahead and get your driver's license at fifteen."

"Me, too," I said. I constantly ran errands for Mother now, and for anyone else who asked me. Mother said I was buying two dollars worth of gas every time she turned around and that the hood of her car never got cooled off. Still, she admitted it was nice not to have to rush out in the car herself every time she ran out of thread.

I pulled into Dr. Power's driveway. He'd had a couple of little pads of concrete laid at an angle to his driveway for patients to park on. He'd bought the old Guice home and established himself an office on one side and living quarters on the other.

I'd met him at church Sunday before last. I was at an age when close-set eyes and a low forehead precluded further interest. He also had bulging veins at his temples. You'd have thought he was Gary Cooper the way the church ladies were all over him — mostly the old maids, like bees on wisteria. It was that way every time a new man came to town. When a busload of soldiers came to church from Camp Van Dorn it was like cracked corn thrown among pullets that hadn't been fed for a week.

Aunt Etta hefted herself out of the car and straightened up. "Oh, my," she said, "look what he's done to Mattie Guice's lawn. What on earth? Well, times change. I guess he had to have some parking space. Well, good gracious, he's taken out Mattie's wood steps and put in concrete. I declare! I don't know about that, now."

I took Aunt Etta's arm as we climbed the steps. Her arm was fat, with deep dimples on either side of her elbow. It felt cool and soft.

"Miss Ruby's not here this afternoon," I reminded her, opening the screened door.

"Well, look a-here," said Aunt Etta, peering around the reception room. "This was Mattie's front bedroom. All those chirren were born right in this room. Well, it's real nice, I reckon. What do we do? Just sit down and wait, I guess."

Aunt Etta got a good grip on the arms of a chair and titanicked into it. I tapped a little silver bell on an oak table by the window. It had an appointment book on it and some papers and a pen and a glossy little wood strip that said *Ruby Burris, R.N.*

In a few minutes Dr. Power opened a door and stepped into the room. He had on a long white coat over his gray trousers. I stood up.

"Dr. Powers, I'm Annie Summerfield, and this is my aunt, Mrs. Maury Summerfield. I made an appointment for her with Miss Ruby for two."

"How do you do, Mrs. Summerfield. Ah, the sore throat," he said, coming over to shake Aunt Etta's hand. I felt sure he was tickled to death to have a new patient. People weren't taking to him too well. He smiled and said, "I'll be with you in just a few minutes. I'm with a patient. But just come this way, you, too, uh, Jane, isn't it? Come right on back. You can be my nurse while Miss Burris is out. How's that?" Aunt Etta struggled up, teetering forward dangerously, I thought, and we followed him down the hall.

"Here we are. You-all just go in and I'll be right there. Jane, you just assist your aunt to get undressed." And he shut the door.

Aunt Etta and I looked at each other. Her mouth and eyes had popped open at the same time.

"Wh . . . what did he say?" she stammered.

"He said for you to undress."

"Lord have mercy! I just want my throat looked at. Of course I won't undress." She looked down at herself. "I should have just gotten a box of Ludens. The idea!" And she sat down in a little chair and began to waggle a black patent pump. She gave a sidelong look at the examining table. It was covered with a crisp white sheet, and a white gown lay folded on it.

"This was Mattie's sewing room. Or it's half of it. He's put a wall down the middle." She fanned herself with a few flaps of her fluted jabot.

"Aunt Etta, I think maybe you ought to undress and put this gown on." I lifted the gown slightly and patted it back down. I looked at her. I couldn't see why she had to undress to have her throat examined. I picked up the cotton gown and flipped it out. Aunt Etta and I both stared at it, the little ironed square folds checkered over it. Both of us were thinking the same thing. This garment would never stretch over Aunt Etta's bosom and at the same time permit her arms to go through the armholes. Whoever made it didn't know everything. It was supposed to lap over in the back with tapes extended to tie it in front.

I heard voices in the hall, so I stuck my head out the door.

"Dr. Power," I interrupted, "my aunt just has a sore throat. She'd rather not undress. She's . . ."

Dr. Power waved a male patient out and said, "What's this? How long has it been since your aunt has had a checkup?"

Aunt Etta heard him, since the door wasn't shut. "Never!" she said. "I have always been perfectly healthy. I just have a little sore throat."

"Come, now, Mrs. Summerfield," Dr. Power said, pushing into

the examining room. "I need to get a full picture—check your heart,
listen to you breathe, check you for lumps. Please, ma'am. Slip out
of your clothes and into that gown for me."

He cut his eyes at me seriously and went into another room across
the hall, the earpieces of his stethoscope clinging to the back of his
neck. I suspected he wanted us to think he had another patient in
there.

I turned back to Aunt Etta. "Well?" I said. "Can I help you?"

Aunt Etta looked down at herself. It occurred to me she probably
hadn't seen her navel in decades. She was about sixty, and Mother
said she'd been topheavy like this since she was young. Got excused
from gym in high school. I felt sorry for her. She probably didn't
want to undress in front of me, much less bare herself before a
strange man. She not only had a record-breaking set of jugs, she
was also an old-fashioned lady.

"Saints preserve us," she said, getting up. And she began to
unbutton the little pearl buttons down the front of her blue crepe.
I helped her pull her dress over her head.

"Wait a minute, honey," she said. "It's hung on my glasses."

I tried to reach under the cloth and get her glasses, which were
hanging on one ear. Her arms were stopped ceilingward in the dress.
I got the glasses loose, finally, and laid them on the examining table.
We pulled the dress off.

Her heavy front bulged even more startlingly in her lace-topped
slip. It made her hips look smaller, and I couldn't help thinking she
looked like a whale. I realized she was not really fat anywhere but
her bosom. Under the arms the slip had six-inch gussets that nar-
rowed near Aunt Etta's hips. Up it came, and I helped her struggle
with it till we got it off. By now her gray hairpins were swinging
loose and her hair was straggling over one eye. We were down to
her corset, something I'd never thought of. Over it she wore some
silk pants that came almost to her knees. Gosh, I thought.

This corset was about the cruelest garment anyone ever could
imagine. She unzipped it and began to undo about a hundred hooks
and eyes down the front. It had her strapped up with vertical stays
that gathered up all the fat in her breasts and propped them nearly

to her chin. It had supporters to her hose on long elastic straps. As she kind of shucked it off, I turned to pick up the gown, not knowing just what we'd do with it.

Aunt Etta was puffing as she sat down to push off her shoes with her feet. Her hose, freed from the supporters, were sagging down over her chubby knees. I didn't want to look at her — or to have her see me looking at her famous body.

I heard her pop the elastic around her waist. "Do you think I have to take off my drawers?"

"I'm not sure," I said.

I spread out the gown and turned around quickly to cover her with it before I could embarrass her. She extended her arms. They went into the armholes about to the elbows, and at that point the gown was full and could be slipped no farther.

"Reckon it'll go on backwards?" she faltered.

"We can try," I said, pulling it away. She turned her back to me and tried to extend her arms backward, groping for the armholes. I pulled the gown on backward, forcing it up to the deep, soft ravine that ran down the middle of her back and into the soft crack between her buttocks. I looked at the ceiling. The gown was on. Backward, but on.

"Aunt Etta, get a hold of those little strings on the edges and pull it closed in front," I said, knowing very well it would never meet in front, much less close.

She turned around. "Lord have mercy, honey. This is without a doubt the most ridiculous predicament I ever got myself into. What in the name of heaven shall we do?" As soon as she turnèd to me I turned away from her, sorting her clothes that lay over the table.

Where was that little fool? Poor Aunt Etta. She stepped up on the low stool to climb onto the table, her stockings about her ankles.

"Here. Take my drawers," she said, sitting on the side of the table and extending her legs. She leaned back on her elbows, the crazy gown gapping, exposing a front view I still managed not to look directly at. I pulled off her drawers and then her stockings and laid them aside.

Suddenly Aunt Etta stood up on the stool. "Take this thing off me," she said, turning her back to me again, in angry resignation.

"For the Lord's sake, take it off. I'm just humiliated. Ruined. I'll just never get over this if I live to be a hundred. If I ever get out of here, I'll move to another state and never show my face here again. Oh, my Lord, nobody must ever hear about this. Not Maury. Not your mother. Nobody."

She sat down hard on the table again and swung her feet up and lay down on her back, naked. Her breasts spread all over her upper body like two flour sacks full of clabber, her saucer-sized nipples like big pale eyes looking out east and west at the same time. Quickly I spread the gown over as much of her anatomy as it would cover, giving priority to breasts and pubic hair. She was breathing heavily, her hair was more askew, and she clutched the sides of the narrow table, her eyes kind of wild, looking at the white ceiling.

Knock, knock. The fool was at the door, opening it before either Aunt Etta or I could say come in.

"Well, now," he sang, "we're all ready? And here's my little assistant."

Who did he think he was, anyway? Jerry Lewis? That's who he reminded me of.

"Doctor Towell, I really can't see why all this was necessary for you to look at my throat . . ."

"All what?" He looked at me and winked. "Listen to her, Janie . . ."

"Annie," I said. We were all losing our minds. I wondered what I could think of to call him. I couldn't beat *Doctor Towell.*

"Annie. Just listen to your mom."

"I'm not her mom. I am her aunt, and I just came in to . . ."

"Quiet now, please . . ." he said, putting a thermometer in her mouth and gripping her wrist. He looked at me and smiled absently.

"All righty. Now." He whipped the gown down to Aunt Etta's navel. I was carefully watching his eyeballs. They rolled in a large square pattern as he took in her bosom. I'd have laid money he hadn't seen anything to compare to my Aunt Etta, even with her lying flat on her back. He jerked his head up for a split second and then began moving his stethoscope about like she was a 32A. He looked pretty casual.

"Yes, yes, yes, yes," he chanted happily as he felt around for lumps. Aunt Etta's knuckles were white as she gripped the table's edge. Then he pulled the gown up. "Now, Mrs. Summerfield, if you'll just slide down and slip your feet into the stirrups, we'll . . ."

Aunt Etta's head raised up, and she looked at him as if she had come upon a mad dog in her zinnia bed. "Young man," she said, rising all the way up to a sitting position, ignoring her gown, which fell across her knees, her lap full of herself, "Young man, the next place my feet are going is back into my shoes. Now, I'll give you another five minutes to look at my throat. Then I'm putting on my clothes and leaving. What in the name of all that's good and holy has happened to the practice of medicine?"

She said more softly, "I just have a sore throat, son."

"Well, now, Mrs. Summerfield. Be calm. So far everything seems fine. If you'd rather have the GYN later, we can wait on that." He quickly slipped a tongue depressor out of a jar, the jar top clinking after him, and laid it on her tongue. "Say ah!"

"Ah-h-gh," choked Aunt Etta.

"Hm-m. Still have those tonsils. Yes, I see a little redness off to the side there. Hold still, now, let me check those ears." He shone his lighted silver cylinder into her ear. "Good. Good. Ears look fine. Fine."

"Now," he said, not so deftly attempting to lift the gown's edge up over Aunt Etta's bosom. She shrugged it away. Let it all show. She no longer cared. The thing was done. This stranger, this young man, had stripped her naked before himself and her niece and exposed her body, the great bosom she had kept covered with restraint and dignity all of her adult life. She was like a good chair with its upholstery torn off.

Doctor Power raised his eyebrows to his low hairline and moved to sit at a little table about the size of a bedtray, where he scrawled out a prescription.

Aunt Etta lay back down and pulled up the gown, more at herself now, modesty returning. Below the knees her blue-veined legs and ankles stuck out coldly, a couple of corns pink on her little toes.

"Here we are," said the doctor. "I'm sorry if I've given you a hard time, Mrs. Summerfield. I know my ways may seem different from what you-all here have been used to with the two older doctors who practiced here for so long. This prescription should clear up the inflammation. And I suggest that you gargle with hot salty water three or four times a day. If you don't feel better by Friday, give us a call." He patted her shoulder and smiled.

"Would you give her a hand, Janie?"

"Annie."

"Excuse me. Annie." He left us.

I helped Aunt Etta pull herself to a sitting position.

"He didn't even charge you," I said, as she hooked up her corset and yanked at the long zipper that covered the hooks and eyes.

"Never fear," she puffed, "Ruby Burris will take care of that." She hooked her stockings to the supporters, twisting to get at the ones in the back. "Lord have mercy. When I bathed and dressed to come down here, I never expected to have to do it all over again." We put the slip, then the dress, over her head. She smoothed everything downward after she buttoned all the little buttons, and I picked up hairpins off the floor, like empty cartridge shells after a battle. I handed her her purse and we left.

Once outside, she gave a big sigh. "I didn't see him as we came out. I guess he had somebody else stripped down in one of those other rooms. If Mattie could see what's going on in her old home, she'd be spinning in her grave. My Lord, I never in all my born days! Just for a little sore throat." She shook her head, looking down at the steps, her white straw handbag swinging on the arm she extended to the railing. "I'm holding on, honey," she said, grasping my arm with her other hand. "I can't bear to think what I could get into here if I broke my leg right here on the little fellow's doorstep." She chuckled. I was glad to hear her sense of humor taking over.

I opened the car door for her, and she backed into the seat and lifted her knees and swung her feet into the car. I slid in beside her and started the car. Aunt Etta looked at me.

"Please stop by the pharmacy, honey, and hand E.J. this prescription. We needn't wait. He'll deliver it."

Aunt Etta was beginning to laugh quietly to herself when I parked at the Blue Tile Pharmacy, and when I came out five minutes later she was laughing too hard to talk. It looked like she was holding her bosom still with her arms.

"Ooh, hoo, hoo, hoo," she shook, "I never . . . I never . . . Ooh, hoo, hoo." She kept laughing till tears rolled off her face and sparkled on her jabot.

I stopped in her driveway.

"Ooh hoo, honey," she gasped, controlling her laughing. With her hand on the door handle she looked at me earnestly. "Promise me you won't tell this on me, Annie." She dabbed at her eyes and blew her nose on her cutwork handkerchief. "Not till I've been dead twenty years. At least." She meant it. The funniness had hit her, but she didn't want anybody else laughing. Not while she was alive, anyway.

She got out and walked around the front of the car. She stopped at the corner of the house by the hydrangea that just matched her dress, the huge blue balls of flowers swelling and ballooning voluptuously all over it. She nodded her head at me. "Promise me?"

"Yes'm," I said, "I promise."

The Visit

I looked out the second-floor window of Sarah Knox Taylor Hall and saw Marcy's car in the graveled driveway. Marcy, a sophomore, lived in Elinor McGehee.

"We're coming," I shouted before she could blow her horn. Betsy was closing her weekend bag. I picked up my own.

"Go on down. I'll be right behind you. Be sure we're signed out, Marianne," she said. We were. She was now fitting her suitcase into a zippered dark blue canvas luggage cover.

When I got down to Marcy's car, she had the trunk open and ready for us to load up. She took my bag and fitted it beside hers, and we stood waiting.

"This is your first visit home with Betsy, isn't it?"

"Yes," I said. "Her mother wrote me the nicest letter inviting me. I can't wait to see the famous Sweet Bay. And to meet Betsy's parents, of course. Wish I could meet her brother. Have you seen the new picture she has of him in his uniform?"

"Have I! You ought to see the real thing." Then she looked serious. "Edgar will be lucky to get out of North Africa alive. Betsy is really calm, him being her only brother and all."

"Escaping from that transport alive proves he's lucky. How many were lost?"

"Thousands. I don't remember. Something incomprehensible. I just hope the war ends before my little brothers are old enough to go." She tossed her keys from one hand to the other. "Betsy's folks are lovely people. You'll be crazy about them." She reached into the

car and blew two loud blasts just as Betsy came around the front
corner of Sarah Knox. She was carrying her suitcase and, over her
shoulder, a dozen or so dresses, hooks of wire hangers around two
fingers.

"I'm coming! I'm coming! I decided to gather up some of these
summer dresses to clear out the closet." She put her small case in
the trunk, then laid the dresses over all the baggage.

"There," she said, and banged the top down.

We got into the car, Betsy in the middle. Marcy spun a little gravel
and drove down the boxwood-lined curves and off the campus, passing under the wrought-iron arch that said *Robert Henry Dabney College for Women 1842,* and in small letters, *Class of 1927.*

Every time I passed under that arch I was a little incredulous. Here
I was a Chicago widow's daughter, a freshman in a girls' college in
Mississippi, of all places. When I found out I'd won the Methodist
scholarship, my friends kidded me.

"Mississippi!"

Getting the scholarship had been easy, but Mom had no money
beyond day-to-day living expenses, and I'd worked all summer at
a nursery, doing all kinds of things, but mostly potting tiny snap-
dragons, chrysanthemums, pinks, and sweet williams to earn myself
some spending money. I now had $42.63 to last till Christmas.
Plenty. I felt very lucky.

I felt especially lucky today to be going home with Betsy. I would
have been embarrassed for her to know what an adventure it seemed
to me.

Betsy's circumstances were completely different from mine. Not
only did she live in a different part of the country, she lived in a
house in a small town. I grew up in Chicago in an apartment, an
only child, with my mother, who became a stenographer to support
us both after my father died. Betsy had twenty-two sweaters, all pull-
overs. She had twelve pairs of shoes. We wore the same sizes in everything except bras, and she constantly offered me her clothes. I had
one thing she liked to wear—my grandmother's plain gold barpin
that had been her graduation present to me.

Today I was wearing my own clothes.

"I don't want your mother to see me come in in your clothes the first time she meets me," I said.

"Aw pooh," said Betsy. "She doesn't care."

But now here we were, uniform, in our box-pleated skirts, saddle oxfords, and baggy sweaters, peter pan dickies, and pearls (mine "simulated," of course), sitting three abreast, tootling down the highway in Marcy's little blue '38 Chevrolet coupé, singing, "I Don't Want to Set the World on Fire" ("I just want to start a flame in your heart").

Betsy elbowed Marcy. "Listen how Marianne says *Fie-yer*," she said. And when I had talked to Mom on the phone last Sunday, she'd said, "Why Marianne, you're already picking up a southern drawl. Listen to that *comin'* and *goin'!*" I couldn't tell. Maybe it was happening. Maybe I would become a Southerner.

I was having a good time. There was constantly something different about being in Mississippi. Since the administrators had lured so many northern girls to the school, field trips were important. We'd been to Biloxi and Vicksburg, and in April we were going to the Natchez Pilgrimage. We had little lectures about the places we were going to visit. Everything seemed to date from the Civil War, seventy-eight years after Appomattox. Oh, yes, Dabney was different from Chicago and our little apartment.

Negro women cleaned the dorms at Dabney and waited on our tables in the dining hall. We could hear them singing in the kitchen, like in the movies. It was all beginning to seem quite real. The woman who waited our table—six of us sat at each round, white-clothed table—was named Iceophene. *Ice-o-phene.* She wore matches in her tight little plaits. One day when she was sweeping the walks around Sarah Knox I stopped a minute with her and asked her where her name came from.

She leaned on her broom, holding it by its top, and said, "Ah-own-nome. Mah mamma ginnit tummy," which Betsy later translated to, "I don't know, ma'am. My mama give it to me."

"Can't you understand plain English?" laughed Betsy.

Sometimes we jitterbugged to records in the spacious end of Winifred Weatherby Dining Hall before dinner, and some of the maids would push open the swinging doors from the kitchen and laugh and clap. They would come over to the ironing room on our floor and "do up" blouses and dresses to make extra change, balling up baskets full of dampened clothes, testing the iron with a wet finger to hear it sizzle ready. I didn't know why I was thinking of Iceophene as we rode down the country highway.

Marcy said, "Y'all have dates tonight?"

"Are you kidding?" Betsy cut her eyes toward me. "No dates in Sweet Bay," and she began to sing, "They're either too young or too old. They're either too gray or too grassy green. The pickin's are slim and the crop is lean. The navy's got the gravy . . ." She trailed off, humming the tune. Two of her high school classmates had been killed since graduation, one in boot camp in California. Betsy had fallen on her bed and cried when she'd received the letter from her mother with the news about both boys.

"No, there's not much to do but talk to my folks and go to church." Then she said in a different tone, "I guess we could go to the electrocution," and her eyes widened briefly before she looked down at her knees.

"Electrocution!" I said. "What are you talking about?"

"I'm not serious about us going, but a Negro is going to be electrocuted tonight, right down in the first-floor hall of the courthouse."

"What did he do?"

"He killed a white man. He wasn't convicted in Daddy's court, but I went down and heard some of his trial. He's guilty. Guilty as homemade sin, they say. And all over ten measly dollars the white man was trying to collect off of him."

"I read about that," said Marcy. "What does your dad say?"

"I think he believes the charge should have been manslaughter. He doesn't say much about it."

"Do you know them?" asked Marcy.

"Oh, sure, I mean I know Abaloyd, and I knew the white man when I saw him. I forget his name."

"Is there an electric chair right in Sweet Bay?" I asked. I pictured the little town to be mostly magnolia trees and azaleas.

"The state has a portable chair that the executioner travels around with," said Betsy. "Lots of states do that. Probably Illinois does."

"Gruesome," I said, looking out at the rolling pastures with trails of creeks and ditches between the soft hills. The October day was clear and the wind that blew our long hair back from our faces felt sweet and clean.

"Cyanide is much more civilized," said Marcy, who had already turned nineteen.

"Everything is so green down here," I said. My mother and I had agreed that we did not believe in capital punishment.

"Yeah," said Marcy. "If we didn't keep hacking away at it, in Louisiana, we'd be living in a jungle in a few weeks. Especially in the summertime."

"Marianne will be seeing Louisiana when we go to the Spring Fiesta."

"Y'all will, maybe, but I'm going home that weekend. What do I want to go to New Orleans for?" said Marcy.

"Why not?" I asked.

"Well, I live so close. I mean I practically live right there, and I can't stand it. It's a filthy, smelly old city with potholes in the streets and drunks all over the sidewalks."

Betsy laughed. "Marcy, what an exaggeration."

Marcy continued, "Don't ever make the mistake of going to Mardi Gras, Marianne. Talk about idiots. It's really stupid."

"Good grief," I said, "I've been dying to go to Mardi Gras."

"Go to Betsy's lynching," said Marcy, "but don't go to Mardi Gras."

"I'm not having a lynching. It's not a lynching. A criminal has been duly convicted and must accept sentence."

"You sound like a judge's daughter," laughed Marcy. She began singing "Smoke Gets in Your Eyes," and we joined in. They knew how to harmonize, and I managed to sing what the glee club director, Miss Pilkington, called second soprano.

Marcy had a sticker on her windshield, *Is This Trip Necessary?* We talked about the war and the shortages of gasoline, tinfoil, sugar, boys, and suddenly we were turning into Betsy's driveway.

Marcy drove to the back and parked alongside a broad tiled terrace.

"Y'all hurry up and get out of here. I've got 'miles to go before I sleep.' " Marcy hopped out and popped open the trunk. "I'll pick you up tomorrow at two o'clock. Be out on the driveway *waiting*. I've got to get back early enough to cram for Old Lady Bosworth's history test Monday morning."

We thanked her for the ride and waved goodbye as she backed around and drove out to the street, where she leaned out and called, "Say hello to your folks."

Betsy's house was remarkably like what I had imagined, only better—big, white, with porches, dark green shutters, wide lawns front and back, magnolias and oaks, and other things that I had already learned to identify: a row of crape myrtles, their little leaves gold, and a bare wisteria twining in thick braids at one corner of the porch. I instantly liked the back yard, heavily bordered with shrubbery, big pots of red geraniums blooming on the terrace like it was July. I wanted to tell Betsy how beautiful I thought it was, but before I could speak a tall white-haired man was striding across the terrace toward us, smiling. He embraced Betsy, saying, "Baby!"

"So this is Marianne," he said shaking my hand. "We're glad to have you, Marianne." He smiled. "Mrs. Cameron and I have been looking forward to meeting Betsy's roommate."

"How do you do, sir. I've looked forward to meeting you."

"Come on in. I'll take these things on up to your room, honey." He managed to carry all of it, dropping a few hangers on the grass, and to open the screened door for us till we were inside the white room, "the porch." I saw it all as with the click of a camera. Terracotta floors, white wicker furniture, bright blue fabrics, two frayed no-color rugs, ceiling fans, ferns on stands in the corners, magazines, books, flowers. I felt myself falling in love with a family and a house as surely as I had, secretly, with the framed face of Edgar that looked at me from Betsy's dressing table at school.

Betsy's mother, Elizabeth, sat on a wicker chaise, her long pretty legs off the side, feet on the floor. She and Betsy looked alike. Mrs. Cameron's hair was short and not so blonde, her face smooth and lightly tanned. I wondered how I looked to her. Her eyes never looked at any part of me but my face. She wasn't looking me over. When I realized that she wasn't, I also realized I must have been fearing . . . what?

"Girls! Marianne, it's good to meet you at last." She reached for my hand with both of hers, holding me for a moment, smiling from one of us to the other. Lying beside her was a newspaper folded to a crossword puzzle.

Betsy kissed her mother. "Hi, Mom. What's wrong? Daddy says you're stove up."

"Oh, nothing worth talking about. I guess I'm destined to carry on my family's taint — arthritis." Smiling at me, with Betsy's smile, she raised her feet to the chaise and sat back against the blue plaid pillows.

"Do you-all need to freshen up before you sit down? Lily will bring you a Coke, or whatever, when you're settled."

Betsy looked at me. "No? Me either. But I'm tired of sitting. Excuse me a minute." I sat down on the blue chintz cushion of the settee, becoming more aware of Mrs. Cameron's obvious delight in having us both there. I looked at the vases of zinnias and shasta daisies, and I was tempted to tell her right there about working at Schlogel's big greenhouses, lifting little seedlings out of flats and into tiny pots.

Then Betsy could be heard from the kitchen. "Lily! Hey! Hey! How've you been? I got the cookies. The whole floor had a feast. What've you cooked up for us tonight? We're starved for something decent. You wouldn't believe the stuff we eat at Dabney. Canned spinach, canned peaches . . ." Then there was low murmuring, and silence.

Mrs. Cameron looked apprehensively through the dining room. "I'm afraid Lily must leave early. You-all can help me warm up supper. She's cooked, and set the table." She nodded toward a wicker card table at the other end of the room, laid with cloth and silver. "But she does have to leave in a few minutes." She looked out the open casement beside her. "I hate to tell you before you've sat down good, but there's something unfortunate going on here tonight that has all the colored people upset. White people, too. We considered asking you-all to wait till another weekend, but you're so busy . . ."

"The electrocution?" I asked, with what I imagined to be my Yankee forthrightness.

"You've heard about it, then."

"Betsy and Marcy were talking about it a while ago. What are the Negroes doing? Do you fear a riot?"

"Oh, good heavens, no, honey. We have the best colored people in this town you'll find anywhere. No. They're holding a big prayer meeting tonight at six up at their Baptist church before this miserable thing at ten. You know—well, maybe you don't know—but colored people are very religious. Very emotional. At preaching they really carry on. They do at funerals, too. Really let go."

I listened to her. No doubt they did. "Is Lily going to the prayer meeting?"

"Indeed she is. Lily is highly respected among her people. A leader. She wouldn't want to stay away. Besides, this colored boy's mother lives next door to her. Poor Lily. She's so upset. This thing is terrible for the whole town. I don't approve of it one bit. It seems so—so uncivilized. They ought to be taken to Parchman if they have to be . . . removed from society."

I fingered the cording of the crisp, glossy chintz on the long cushion that I was sunk down in in the middle of the settee.

"The boy's mother thinks Lily should be able to get the Judge to call the governor and ask for a stay."

"Could he do it?"

"It wouldn't do a bit of good. In the first place, the boy is guilty of killing that man, just as guilty as homemade sin, but he wouldn't plead guilty. He had a fair trial."

"But maybe guilty of manslaughter and not murder . . ."

"Well, Ned—Judge Cameron—has said that—privately. I guess Betsy told you." She picked up the fountain pen that she'd clipped to the folded newspaper and began tapping it against the crossword puzzle. "You see, this white man, actually not a person of much substance, went to the boy's house—his name is Abaloyd; they do come up with some names, don't they?" I thought of Iceophene. "This man, Mixon, stepped up on the porch to collect some back rent—ten dollars, I think. Don't take that lightly; it was probably a week's pay for Abaloyd. Well, he'd been there several times trying to get his money. It was night, and Abaloyd says he thought this Mixon was carrying a gun—apparently it was a flashlight—and he says he was trying to protect his family. He has a wife and a houseful of

little pickaninnies, of course — and he panicked, he said. And, well,"
she lifted her shoulders and her eyebrows in a harmonious shrug,
"well, he blew this Mixon to kingdom come. Mixon had told several
people that Abaloyd had threatened him on his earlier calls for the
rent on the house. So there you are." She sighed. "Who knows? Abaloyd testified that Mixon wouldn't fix the roof or the flue and that
he had done work on the cabin worth twice his back rent." She patted
her lap with the paper. "I'm just glad it wasn't in the Judge's court.
It would have worried him to death. He is a very compassionate
man." She looked at the ceiling, then at me with her steady eyes.
"I do feel sorry for the poor things."

I was not sure what she was saying or why. I did know that I liked
her. She was just like Betsy. Open. The similarity of their smiles was
eerie. For me. I was just as taken, as Betsy would have said, with
the Judge — *Ned,* undoubtedly *Edgar.* They were lovely people, as
Marcy had said in the driveway at Dabney.

Betsy came back eating an apple. "Want a bite?" She held the apple
out to me.

"Betsy! Offer Marianne a whole apple, not one you've been eating
on."

"Oh, that's all right," I said, taking a quick bite. It was so rich
and sweet that I took a second, larger bite.

"Germs, germs, germs," said Betsy's mother, looking at the puzzle.

"Lily's all upset about Abaloyd. She says his mother thinks Daddy
ought to try calling the governor."

"Darling, you know he would if he thought it would do any good,
or would do no harm — was right and proper. But the governor and
your father are barely on speaking terms. I can tell you he couldn't
get that man to save his own mother."

Betsy swung her foot, chewed, and looked at the remaining side
of her apple. "Well, I . . ."

"What on earth is a four-letter book of the Bible? It isn't *Amos.*
The third letter is definitely *t.*"

"*Acts?*" suggested Betsy.

"Of course! Betsy, you make me feel . . . !" And she began filling
in the letters.

Judge Cameron came back. "Want a Coke? Where's Lily, hon?"

He looked toward the kitchen. "Let me get you-all some pop. Want it on ice? I like Coke in the bottle." He smiled at me, crowfeet spreading toward his temples. "Has more fizz."

"Ivanhoe maiden?" said Mrs. Cameron, not looking up.

"Rowena," I said.

"See, I told you she was smart," laughed Betsy. "You ought to ask her some on Greek myths."

"I rely on your daddy for Greek and Latin. But, Betsy, I clearly remember giving you a child's book of myths years ago, the same time I gave you Lamb's *Tales from Shakespeare* . . ."

Betsy's father was back quickly with Cokes in little knit coasters. He held three bottles among the fingers of both hands. "There we go."

"Thank you," I said.

"Thanks, Pop," said Betsy.

"No, thank you, Ned," said Mrs. Cameron. "You drink it. I had one just before the girls arrived."

The Judge turned up the Coke bottle and chug-a-lugged half of it. "Ah-h-h," he exhaled. "Lily has had them up on the ice trays for twenty minutes. Perfect!"

"Betsy, we got a V-mail from Edgar yesterday. I put it on your dresser so you can read it. It took less than a week to get here." She smiled at Betsy and began putting some letters on her puzzle. The Judge looked at his wife, but she didn't look up. I could feel the apprehension they shared. I could imagine them vowing not to ruin Betsy's visit with her roommate at home by talking about the expected invasion of Italy and their fears for their son. I looked at his picture in a silver frame sitting on a long table. It was like the one Betsy had at school. He looked like his father—as much as Betsy looked like her mother.

"Lily's after me again. Abaloyd's mother is about to drive her crazy. I can't help them. If intervention were indicated, I'd intervene, or try to, but it's all over and done with. And the governor wouldn't listen to me under any circumstances. He can't forgive me for not supporting him. And he knows that if he runs for the Senate, I won't support him for that." He stood up and rubbed the back of his neck and gazed far into the back yard, where a tire hung on a knotted rope from an oak limb.

"Now, Ned, I don't want you upset. Sunday this will all be over and they'll settle down. What's a five-letter word for South American mount — oh, my heavens, *Andes,* of course. I almost made a fool of myself again. What's the matter with me?" She laughed.

"I'd say not much if you can work one of those things in ink. That's confidence, isn't it, Marianne?"

"Optimism, I think it is," said Betsy.

"I'm a puzzle addict myself," I said. "I'm amazed at how much better I am with one in the morning than I am at night." I meant it.

"My goodness, I thought that was age with me. It's true. But, yes, an addict is what I am, I guess. There is nothing, absolutely nothing, more relaxing," said Elizabeth Cameron, looking up at her son's picture.

"Come on back to the kitchen, Marianne. I want you to meet Lily before she has to leave. She probably won't be here in the morning." Betsy gathered up the empty Coke bottles.

"Does she work on Sunday?" I asked.

"'Course. That's when we need her the most. We'd never get off to church or have any dinner when we got home if it weren't for Lily. She's spoiled us for too long." Betsy led me into the dining room and, through a swinging door, into a breakfast room and the kitchen.

A small gray-haired, gray-uniformed woman was at work with a rolling pin on biscuit dough that was spreading a little more with each light pass of the pin. She had flour up to her wrists, and she moved quickly.

"This is Marianne, Lily. This is Lily, Marianne." Betsy was smiling. She picked up a few last scraps of dough and began rolling them into a ball with rotating motions of her palms.

"We glad to have you, Miss Marianne," said Lily, setting her rolling pin in a big wooden bowl of flour and looking at me carefully. Her eyes were light hazel. "We hear a lot about you. You keepin' this girl out of trouble?"

"Hello, Lily," I said, self-conscious about calling this elderly, dignified woman by her first name. She began cutting biscuits with the floured rim of a little cheese glass, quickly stamping them and lifting them onto a greased cookie sheet.

"Now, Miss Betsy, you just shove these in the oven. Remember, 425, and keep an eye on 'em after ten minutes. Don't put 'em in till you've got everything else about ready. Heat up the butterbeans on low and the rice and the gravy. They're all sittin' right there. Y'daddy likes cold chicken, but if you-all want it warm, put it in the oven befo' you bake y'biscuits, and keep it covered."

"Don't worry, Lily. We'll manage. I've got a real cook here to help me. Marianne's mother works, and they don't even have a cook. She can probably run the whole show." She said it with genuine admiration. She flattened the ball into a biscuit and dropped it on to the pan. "Has Mother been feeling really bad?"

"Well, you know how it is. She *will* work in that yard. I'd fall right down dead if I did what she does out there. Judge, he can't do nothin' with her. Jake, he's playin' out. She mainly got her boy on her mind, but she keep so quiet about it. I think her worries break out in her back. She need to let go a little bit, really let go." Lily looked at me. "Are you from Deetroit, honey?"

"No, Chicago."

"Oh, that's right. You a long way from y'mama. Do you miss her?"

"I'll say," I told her, "but I'll see her at Christmas."

"That won't be long. Time'll fly. Jesus knows how I'd love to be with my mama, just one hour." Lily was scrubbing the biscuit board, the tabletop, sink, and all the utensils. She filled the drain basket. She shook her head over the sink.

"Law' have mercy, how I wish the Judge could help po' Mattie. She's about crazy over her boy. Abaloyd killed that white man. But Law', if they could just put him in the pen and let him live." She shook her head again. "He's a good boy, too. Never been a minute's trouble. Help Mattie all along. We never had an execution here ever that I know anything about. I just don't see why they have to start now."

The Judge pushed through the swinging door. "Lily, you can go on home when you want to. You've got to get to prayer meeting, and it's getting late. Want Betsy to take you home?"

"Yessuh. That'd be nice. Oh, Judge, if you could only stop this thing. You gon' feel bad when you walk in that courthouse Monday mornin', knowin' what happen there at ten o'clock tonight."

"Lily! I already feel bad. We've been all over this. I tell you it is out of my hands, never was in my hands." He leaned toward her, his hands, palms up, emphasizing his words. "The governor wouldn't listen to me. You just don't understand politics."

Lily took off her white apron and wiped her eyes. "Po' Mattie," she said. "They should have charged Abaloyd with manslaughter, not murder."

"I'll get the keys," said Betsy, patting Lily's shoulder. "Want to come, Marianne?"

"Sure," I said. And we went out the back door to the garage, where we each pushed open a door. Lily got into the back seat of the dark sedan, and Betsy and I got into the front.

We drove through several shady streets under oaks that were thick and green, past houses that sat far back from the street. Every house had a porch, some screened.

"This is a pretty town," I said.

I was surprised at how quickly we were stopping to let Lily out. After driving no more than three blocks, we had turned into a street of packed, rutted red clay. It was lined with unpainted cottages, shacks. Most of the houses had outside, roughly built chimneys, board and batten walls, and, on the side of each screenless window, a single shutter made of boards. Somewhere along the back of each small lot was a privy. Negro children played among dogs that ambled or jumped and barked. The chickens pecked at the bare clay or fluttered this way and that in the wake of dogs and children. Some boys were knocking a rusty can around with sticks made from limbs. They screamed and laughed and ran in front of the car as if they did not see us.

Lily gathered up several brown paper bags, grease-spotted, tops tightly twisted, and two *Time* magazines. She also had a garment over her arm.

"Honey, I didn't say goodbye to y'mama. I don't think I ever did such a thing befo'. You tell her I 'preciate this dress. I'm gon' wear it tonight. Now you thank her, babygirl."

It was a cream-colored crepe dress. I wondered how she could make it wearable by six o'clock. Mrs. Cameron was five or six inches taller than Lily. Lily shut the door and headed for a house that was somehow a little sturdier, neater than the others. It had an unpainted picket fence. The gate was held closed by a circle of rope, and a cowbell on a piece of chain rattled unmelodiously when she pulled the gate closed behind her. We watched her go up two plank steps and across the porch, which was lined with Crisco cans filled with lush green ferns and geraniums. She pushed the door open with her foot and went in.

Betsy drove the big car back onto a beautiful street and I thought of my neighborhood on the north side of Chicago, Rogers Park, and the dark Germanic look of the big apartment buildings, and of my mother there, comfortable, at home, and of me here, feeling curious but not alien. And I thought of Lily in her house wallpapered with Sunday comic pages, so Betsy said, Gasoline Alley, Ella Cinders, Andy Gump, Moon Mullins, all around her while she readied a dress for tonight with a waistline that hung to her skinny bottom, its hem around her ankles.

"That's our church," Betsy said, pointing to a neat New England-like little white church with a green lawn and green shutters with Gothic points.

"I'll bet I know what that big yellow brick one is over there: Baptist."

"Don't you know it."

"I still can't get over how much like summer it is, and practically November."

"I know. I love it like this. Not hot. Not cold. Sometimes we hardly have any winter at all. But then other years we have long spells of a week or more of freezes at night. When I was in the fifth grade it snowed in late March. You should have seen it. Everybody went wild. The schools closed. Stores, too. We made sleds and snowmen and snowballs. I'll never forget Mother waking me up early and saying, 'Betsy, look out the window,' and there it was, all that pure white, covering everything. Everything. It looked like the whole world had somehow been purified. Mrs. Anderson down the street from us wouldn't let us kids on her lawn because she didn't want her snow tracked up."

"That is funny."

"Within twenty-four hours it was all slush, except for shady places, where the snow hung on for several days. I wish it would snow this winter, at school. Wouldn't that be fun?"

"I guess so." I was thinking of Rogers Park again and how quickly the snow got gray and dirty.

I helped Betsy push the garage doors closed, and she connected the hasp, but there was no padlock.

When we came into the back hall that ran on through the middle of the house, Betsy suddenly held me back and put her finger against her lips. She nodded toward the phone cord leading into the closet under the stairs. We could barely hear the Judge's voice. "I know, Governor . . . but, he's never . . . manslaughter . . ."

Elizabeth Cameron came into the hall. "Girls, why don't you hang up your clothes? Marianne hasn't even been upstairs, Betsy."

We ran up the back stairs. "I'll be! Wait!" We stopped in the hall. A door closed below. "Listen!" she said.

"Would he even come to the phone, Ned?"

"The old bastard let me talk my head off, really beg, before he told me he'd granted a stay a few minutes ago. He's going to review the transcript, he said. That boy will never go to the chair."

"I hope you're right, honey." They were quiet for what seemed like a long time to me as we stood there listening.

"Let me run up to Lily's and let her know," he said. "She can locate Mattie if nobody else has, and I doubt they have." We heard the door shut and, after a bit, the car start.

Betsy's room was big, the prettiest bedroom I'd ever been in. Her mahogany four-poster was so high it had steps, and her big walnut dresser had matching ivory everything, even a nail buffer, all mono-grammed in swirly script, initials not her own. I loved the room.

"Here," she said, handing me a satin hanger. And we hung up our church dresses.

"That's the bathroom. You can go first, since you're company — process that Coke."

I went into the bathroom and closed the door. I closed a door into the hall and turned to one that opened on another bedroom, a man's room. Edgar's. Two golf bags leaned heavily against a walnut armoire, club heads pressed against dark wood like long-necked birds, listening, waiting. A bookcase held rows of trophies, little pedestaled golden men in peaked caps, drivers swung back, swift strokes frozen. There was no dust anywhere. My eyes played briefly over the rest of Edgar's room before I closed the door with a heavy metallic click.

The bath was white, a room as big as our kitchen in Rogers Park, tiled as high as my head, fixtures gleaming as though they'd never known abrasive cleaner. I sat down, thinking that the furnishings of this house, like its people, knew only gentle care. After I flushed the toilet and washed my hands, I walked back into the bedroom, smoothing my skirt down.

Betsy was folding the little V-Mail. She stuck it under the edge of the clock on the mantel. "Great letter," she said, and she thumped the glass over the clock's face. "This is a perfectly good old clock. It's stopped because I stopped it. The day Edgar left from his last leave home, I decided I would stop it, and when he comes home, I'm going to start it up again. He and I will come up here and wind it up and start that pendulum swinging again. Does that sound silly?"

"Good grief, no. I think it's a wonderful idea. Does he know you stopped it?"

"Yeah. He and I came up here, and I showed him. Edgar's six years older than I am, but he never shows it if he thinks I'm silly. He's a real peach."

"Well, he certainly looks it." I sighed, looking at his picture.

"Yeah, that, too." She smiled at me.

I looked around the room. "Betsy, how do you stand living in Sarah Knox?"

"I like it. I like the idea of it being a hundred years old. I know what you mean, but I like it, rats and all. It's not as bad as camp. Well, it's kind of like camp for inconvenience. But it's dry," she laughed.

"I like it, too, the history, but for comfort, it's a far cry from home."

"I'll tell you what," she said, tossing her sweater on a chair, "I really love this room. It's always been my cocoon. I'd hate to think I'd ever be unable to come back to it." She laughed. "This house has been here since 1880, so I guess it's not going to get up and walk off."

God, I thought, they're all so comfortable. And so *nice*. Not too nice, either. They really are nice. Judge Cameron calling the governor was almost too much, and then going to tell Lily.

"Girls!" Judge Cameron was back and halfway up the back stairs. "It's nearly five. Want to go down and meet Number 3?"

I looked at Betsy, puzzled.

"Oh, let's do. Yeah, Dad! We'll be right down. Come on." She grinned. "Now get ready, Chicago. Meeting Number 3 is uptown."

"Is it a train?" I had ridden down to school on a number something.

"That's what it is. You'll see." We hastily pulled our sweaters back on and brushed our identical hairdos — long and straight to the shoulders and turned up on the ends, the front pulled smoothly to one side with a barrette. But my hair was dark.

As we raced down the stairs Betsy said, "You may see some boys after all. Soldiers!"

At the bottom of the stairs she said, "I know you called the governor, Pa." I never heard the matter of Abaloyd mentioned again that weekend, even by Lily, who was singing "Jesus, Lover of My Soul" in the kitchen when I waked up early the next morning.

Betsy's mother had started another puzzle that she said she had saved from last Sunday's *Times-Picayune*. She straightened her back and walked with little evidence of pain. "I hope you don't think I just sit around doing nothing but work crossword puzzles, Marianne. They are sort of soothing while I'm out of commission. I'm getting pretty tired of the role of disabled lady."

"You've got to stay out of those flowerbeds, Elizabeth. You should use some of that energy on the golf course with me." He had his arm around her waist.

The Judge drove us in the dark sedan through the streets of Sweet Bay.

"There's the courthouse, Marianne. Look. Down there." And there it was, a confusion of styles, Greek Revival the most insistent because of the massive columns. HOLDEN COVNTY COVRT HOVSE was carved in the entablature. It sat back a hundred yards from the street, a broad brick boxwood-bordered walk leading to the double french doors. In the ebbing light the windows were black and still, reflecting nothing of the history it must have seen, today and other days for decades.

"It's very handsome," I said.

"And this is Main Street," said Betsy. We drove past a block of one- and two-story buildings with a variety of shelters over the sidewalks. Storefronts—a bank, groceries, a drugstore, Straus's Café.

"Most of these folks are country people in town for their Saturday shopping," Judge Cameron said of the men, women, and children walking about and sitting in cars and trucks. We bumped across the tracks; then the Judge turned the car around and parked on the bricked area beside the station, facing the double tracks of the Illinois Central. We couldn't see the town across the tracks where we'd come from because of the dense and glistening magnolia trees that grew in the hedged park along the Main Street side of the railroad. Another car was already parked, and some others soon came and lined up with us. The Judge got out and walked to the corner of the station. He took his watch out of his vest pocket and looked first at it, then at the blackboard on the station wall.

Pushing his watch into his pocket, he walked back to the car and looked in at us. "Five minutes late."

"This is an entertainment in Sweet Bay," Betsy explained to me. "The train heads out of New Orleans in the afternoon and gets into Chicago in the morning, early. Number 4 comes down in the morning, passes through here about seven-thirty . . ."

"Seven-forty," said her mother, not looking up from her puzzle.

"Well, you can get to New Orleans on Number 4 just as the stores are opening on Canal Street, shop a couple of hours, have lunch at Holmes or Arnaud's or somewhere nearby—the gumbo and soft-shelled crabs at Gluck's are good—and then you can shop a little more and get home on Number 3. It sure beats that car trip through the swamp. I hate that road. Mother and Daddy have been driving it for so many years they don't seem to notice. It's so wavy it makes me sick. You'll see, come April."

"Betsy! The way you exaggerate," said her mother.

"We're lucky the trains stop here. They used to stop down at Chitamawa, but every time they stopped, the people climbed on the train and drank up all the ice water." She was laughing and looking at me to see if I fully appreciated her joke. "Now the trains go through there so fast they flush every toilet in town!"

"*All three,*" quoted her mother. "Daddy will have to start copyrighting his jokes," she laughed. "Are you amused, Marianne?"

"Yes," I laughed. It was funny. The image of a train rushing hell-bent through a tiny town, causing "all" the toilets to flush was funny.

The Judge joined several other men near the station. One man walked out and stood between the tracks, his hands in his pockets, and stared south.

"Here she comes," he called.

"Howard, get off those tracks!" called a woman from the car next to us. The man looked her way and stayed where he was long enough to make it clear he wasn't taking orders. Then he joined the Judge and the others, all looking south. Most of the women sat in the cars.

I saw the diamond-bright light as it pierced the haze far down the straight track. Twice the whistle blew long warning blasts as it approached crossings. The engine reached us after what seemed a long time and then passed, braking and screeching, the bell ringing.

A man pulled a wagon away from the station and was hurrying after the baggage car. Several coaches filled with soldiers passed us, boys in khaki crowded at the windows. A girl about our age sat on the fender of a car, and the soldiers waved to her and grinned, as if they expected to see her again. She swung her legs and smiled and waved till they were too far up the track for her to see them anymore.

When the train stopped with a gnash and groan of brakes and whoosh of steam, a conductor stepped down in front of us and placed the squat, sturdy stool on the crushed rock. With his white cloth he wiped the handrails, and then he began helping passengers down. Mostly shoppers from New Orleans, I guessed, and several soldiers who got off the coach.

"Mother, look! There's Clifton Terry. He was with Edgar at Tulane." She put her head out the window and called, "Hey, Clifton! Welcome home!" He smiled and waved but hurried the other way to meet a middle-aged couple who hugged him till his overseas cap fell to the ground. A boy of about ten picked up the cap and put it on his own head and grinned.

I looked up and down the length of the long train. Farther up the track some soldiers and civilians were getting off the all-Negro coach behind the baggage car.

Back toward the end of the train one man stepped down out of a Pullman and stood waiting alone, leaning on a furled umbrella as though it were a cane, a rolled newspaper under his arm.

"Al Marshall," said Mrs. Cameron, when she sensed I was looking at him. I had the feeling of receiving privileged information.

"Who is he?"

"He's a bum," said Betsy.

"Whatever else he may be, he isn't a bum, Betsy." She began to address me. "He's just a local man who held onto his money and property when everyone else was suffering during the Depression, by putting everything he had in the name of his wife and daughter."

"What about that Negro property he had that he burned for insurance?"

"Betsy! You never heard that from me. Or your father!"

Betsy nudged me. "It'll take more than a few weekend visits here for you to even begin to learn about the characters in this town."

"I'm curious to know about them," I said, honestly.

"I'll bet you there isn't one town in Illinois as full of loonies as this one. Every house has somebody in the attic."

"Betsy, for goodness sake. All small towns are just alike. I've told you that." Mrs. Cameron cleared her throat. "What's a four-letter word meaning *glacial ridge?*"

"What've you got?" asked Betsy.

"Nothing, so far."

"I can't help you."

"It just gets me when they put in a word like that. Now who on earth would know that? *Units of work;* that's easy — *ergs.*"

"Speaking of dumb words," said Betsy.

Her mother looked down at her puzzle most of the time we sat there meeting Number 3, but when she looked up she knew what was going on, who was meeting whom.

Then we saw a pine box, a coffin, being brought through the wide baggage-car opening. A spic-and-span colored soldier was shaking hands with several people; then he helped some men move the box down our way and onto the back of a flatbed truck.

Mrs. Cameron leaned forward to look. "Some colored boy," she said. We could see people come and stand close to the back of the truck. A woman was weeping, having to be supported. The soldier turned to her and removed his cap and laid his hand on her shoulder, and she looked up at him, her face twisted in soft brown lumps of sorrow.

"I don't recognize any of those colored folks," said Betsy, stepping out onto the running board and looking over the top of the car.

"Betsy! Get back in this car. It's rude to stare at them like that. We'll have to remember to watch the colored service column in next week's paper. They're from out in the country." Her voice sounded strained.

Then more lightly she said, "Whistle your father on over here. We don't need to be sitting here after the train is gone. We've got to get home and get supper on the table. The oven has to heat up. And you girls must be starved." She watched as the truck turned around and pulled off in the opposite direction. Some pine boughs had been laid on the top of the coffin.

"Poor things," said Mrs. Cameron to herself. For a moment, I knew she was quite alone.

Betsy got out of the car again and, placing two fingers on her lower lip, emitted an ear-splitting whistle. Mrs. Cameron and I both jumped.

"Betsy! Good heavens! I didn't mean for you to sound an alarm. What's the matter with you, anyway?" But she was laughing.

Betsy leaned down and looked into the car, grinning. "Well, you said to whistle."

Without turning, the Judge casually waved a hand in our direction. One of the men was talking earnestly. After a moment the Judge quickly shook hands with the men and walked toward us. "I'm glad you haven't forgotten everything your big brother taught you," he said, standing close beside Betsy.

She hung her wrist over his shoulder and watched the train, which was rolling slowly now. She was watching as intently as if it were a serious drama on a stage, as if she had never seen a train depart from a station before. The diner came at a leisurely pace before us, its long windows glowing in the dusk, like a passing gallery of big illuminated photographs, showing the white linens, gleaming silver, glassware, the profiles of people facing each other over the tables.

Outside, at the back of the diner, a plump middle-aged waiter stood, his crisp white jacket buttoned up to his chin, his hands braced against the half-door over the coupling. Betsy raised her arm high and waved her hand to him. She smiled, her mouth open. And the waiter, seeing her, quickly flashed white teeth in a big warm smile and raised his arm and waved to her, his fingers spread wide, as if he had counted five.

They waved and waved and waved, till all we could see of him was a white speck far, far up the track, heading into the all-night run to Chicago.

The Peaceful Eye

The pecan leaves didn't crackle under her saddle oxfords as they might have on a warm, clear October morning. The rain last night had made them soggy. She felt a need for a crisp response beneath her shoes, and the little corner of her mind that was aware of these things told her that the magnolia leaves up in front of the Gatchells' would be crunchy. It took more than a night's rain to soften them, and this gave her a half-conscious comfort. They would jigsaw into little brown geometrics and lie there until barely larger than grit. She kicked a pecan, still in its bright green outer shell. It smacked sharply against a tree and glanced off into the gutter, where it lay bruised and immature on the concrete.

I promised myself I'd never go to Miss Emma's again. I wish I could turn back. But Miss Scott would wonder why. And I'm the only one in the class who knows where her rooms are. She'd think I was crazy.

It was just after morning recess when Miss Scott asked her to run an errand. Civics class was about to begin, and Mary had spent recess memorizing the names of the President's cabinet: John Nance Garner, Henry Wallace, James Farley . . . Mary gave no thought to what the errand might be. Miss Scott knew she liked to get out of class to do most anything except dust erasers.

She laid her yellow Mikado pencil in the long narrow slot on her desk with the point right at the J. of J.V.B. that someone had carved there long ago. Then she walked up to the teacher's desk with the envious eyes of twenty sixth-graders on her back.

"Mary, I forgot my grade book. Would you mind walking up to Miss Emma's to get it?"

"Yes ma'am. I mean, no ma'am. I'll go. Where'll I find it?"

"Just look in my room on the bed or the dresser. I'm sure it's out where you'll see it. I'll appreciate it, honey." She smiled.

Mary knew all about Miss Scott's apartment. Miss Emma Lamar's house was across the street from her own, and Mary knew where Miss Scott kept most of her things. She knew what books were in the bookshelf, where the alarm clock sat beside the yellow bread-box on the oilcloth-covered table in the tiny kitchen, and how the three little fringed pillows were lined up on Miss Scott's bed that was covered with the white chenille bedspread. Mary's favorite thing in the whole apartment was a perfume bottle of delicate pink frosted glass that sat on the white linen lace-edged dresser scarf. Miss Scott had once pulled out the long glass stopper and touched her white wrists, where the veins were blue. She assured Mary her beating pulse forced the scent into the air about her. Mary tried this with some of her mother's perfumes, and she felt that it worked, but she couldn't find a scent on her mother's crowded dressing table that was as heavenly as Appleblossom.

Miss Scott wasn't Miss Scott anymore. She was Mrs. Fite. Last year she had married Billy Fite, a fat little meatcutter who cried and called his mother when it lightninged. Everyone in town knew about that. Billy was a butcher—a butcher! Everyone called him a meat-cutter. It somehow sounded better—almost artistic. Billy wore a bloody apron, and Mary had watched him cleave the largest joint of a cow with one blow of that great axe-like knife. It was a splendid and terrifying performance, and Mary knew that Billy put his heart and soul into that blow. Afterward he would strike the surface of the square block of a tree that was his table and leave his meat axe vibrating while he wiped his hands on his blood-browned apron. He had a sweet shy smile.

Now Mary zigzagged so she could step on the big magnolia leaves and at the same time avoid the lines of the sidewalk.

"I hope Miss Emma's not at home, so I won't have to see her." Realizing she had spoken out loud, she looked around to see if anyone might have heard her, but no one was near. For a moment she walked straight, heedless of crackling leaves or the lines that would make her a rotten egg if she stepped on them.

Miss Scott had asked her why she never came to see her anymore. But Mary couldn't tell her why — that something too terrible to describe had happened between her and Miss Emma — that she felt she never could look at Miss Emma again, much less run the risk of talking to her.

Miss Scott was tall and looked like a Spanish queen. She wore her dark hair parted in the middle and pulled back into a low full bun on her neck. Not one bit of her ears showed, and her hair shone like Sunday shoes. She had jaws like Joan Crawford's — square, with hollow cheeks. Her eyes were large and dark with thick, straight black lashes that looked like starched fringe. Mary had studied them, and she'd decided that they were too stiff to yield to the eyelash curler that her sister used to turn up her light brown lashes. The most fascinating thing about Miss Scott's face was her dark moustache which could fill Mary with a mixture of revulsion and awe. Once, Miss Scott had bleached it, only to have the most horrible yellow moustache glowing like a Mardi Gras joke on her proud face. But the moustache didn't really bother Mary.

Miss Scott had married Billy because she was thirty and figured he was her only chance. How many grown people had Mary heard say that? He was a foot shorter than she was, and he was a mama's boy, but he did come from a nice family, and Miss Scott seemed happy with him. Mary wondered if Miss Scott had ever seen Billy at work at McGraw's Market, where he hacked and sawed and sliced his way through cow after cow and pig after pig.

Miss Emma's house was only four blocks from school, and Mary could have made the trip blindfolded because she walked to and from school twice every day — she went home for lunch. Everybody went home for lunch in Sweet Bay, only it was dinner in the middle of the day. Myrt cooked a big dinner every day, and at night Mary had a light supper. It was only when they stayed in a hotel in New Orleans that Mama called the night meal *dinner*. And that was because it *was* dinner. In New Orleans all meals were dinners, and Mama and Daddy would try to be polite with their belching on the way home while Mary sat on the back seat of the car counting turtles on floating logs in the canal. Between LaPlace and Pontchatoula she would sometimes count over a hundred. After dark she counted one-eyed cars. The swamp road was wavy, and Daddy drove fast. She would stare ahead at the road lighted by the headlights, trying not to think of the deep black water on either side of the highway.

Mary ran her hand along the tops of the fence pickets as she walked past Mrs. Gatchell's. Mrs. Gatchell was sitting on her front porch with a large blue and white enameled bowl on her lap. She was picking over mustard greens and rocking. Her heels came down rhythmically as she discarded the tough ends of the greens on a newspaper beside her chair. "Morning, Mary. Playing hookey?" Mary said no.

The Gatchells had a concrete platform in front of their gate on the edge of the street. It was made for stepping into a carriage or mounting a horse. Now it was just something to scratch the paint off a car door. It had a slab of white marble in the top of it with *Gatchell* set in blue tile letters. Last Halloween some high school boys had painted out the *Gatc* with green paint, leaving *hell*. Mrs. Gatchell was outraged, and she found out that Bud Carnes and Mickey Beaumont did it and made them clean the paint off. Mary looked at it now. Faint traces of green paint showed in the concrete around the marble. She looked at Mrs. Gatchell and her blue bowl of greens and her skinny ankles that showed below her housedress. She liked to think of her out there standing over Bud and Mickey, threatening to call their parents if they didn't scrub and scrape harder. Mrs. Gatchell was tough, but she wasn't crazy. Miss Emma was. Mary liked a lot of old people in Sweet Bay whom she regarded as a little odd. Old Mr. Dickerson really believed his house was haunted by the man who built it before the Civil War. That was fun. But Miss Emma was something else.

Mary had thought Miss Emma was just different, and she liked her. *My friend Miss Emma.* For one thing she was a Yankee, and the way she pronounced her r's made Mary think of biting hard candy. Mary used to spend hours in Miss Emma's porch swing, her toes barely scraping the clean gray-painted floor. As she swung gently back and forth, her fingers would travel up and down the links of chain, and she and Miss Emma talked about all sorts of things. The porch faced east and was lovely and shaded in the afternoons—in the spring fragrant with wisteria and magnolia fuscatas humming with bumblebees — in the fall when the air changed so mysteriously and the smell was of burning leaves and acorns, and the grassless spots under the big oak in front of the porch were traced with the finely combed trails of the leaf rake. She remembered the good croquet games they used to have. But all of this ended for Mary months ago.

Miss Emma's house was a two-story cottage with banistered porches upstairs and down. Her house sat to one side of the property, and she had a big side lawn that was flat enough for croquet. It sloped off near the street corner where there was a great cedar with the ground underneath covered with ivy and fern, and to Mary it had been a wonderful place. Miss Emma's yard was surrounded by hedges — low boxwood up near the house but an eight-foot privet down by the cedar, to screen off the Negro quarter which started right across the street.

The first Negro house belonged to Jim Cannon. Jim had a wooden leg and a moustache. He smoked a corncob pipe, and he was an expert at trimming hedges. He once told Mary that his shears were his "living." Mary had never forgotten, and after that she noticed he always carried his shears under his arm. His empty pantsleg was packed in neat folds between the wooden leg and his stump. Jim's own hedge was as high on Miss Emma's side as hers was on his. His was very fancy, with higher squares at the corners and at his gate. In one side he had sculptured a bench with arms, but you couldn't sit in it. Mary had tried. The sharp, stubby branches had scratched her when she sat on the soft-looking green foliage. It was like jumping into a big pile of leaves expecting to plop down on a cushiony heap and landing with a shocking thud on the hard ground beneath. You couldn't tell how hard something was by looking at it.

Miss Emma was a Methodist and a widow. She walked to church every Sunday in good weather. When it rained she rode with Mary's family or with Miss Phaedra Mullins, another neighbor. Miss Emma was thin as a slat, with a pale little face, and she wore only white powder for makeup — no lipstick even. Mary always noticed that. She wore beige or brown, and in the summer she sometimes wore white. Now she reminded Mary of a dead mouse in a trap, especially when Miss Emma stood singing in the choir, her mouth dropped open just like the mouse's, chin receding. She was so like that mouse that lay dead on the storeroom floor. But Miss Emma hadn't been to church lately.

She used to play bridge almost every night except Sunday, which would have been a sin. She played with her two upstairs roomers, "those two pansies." Mary had pictured the bridge foursome in Miss Emma's sitting room, Miss Emma and two large gold and purple velvet pansies and somebody else for a fourth — Miss Phaedra sometimes. Miss Scott used to play with them before she married. Now she and Billy spent every night in their rooms with the shades down, and the mouse and the two pansies had to call someone — when they played, which was hardly ever now. Silky playing bridge didn't sound any sillier than two pansies. Silky was Miss Emma's golden spaniel.

Mary stopped and put her foot up on the red fire hydrant and tied her shoe. Silky was dead. She walked on.

When Miss Emma sang in the choir her lips never changed shape. Her jaw just worked up and down. She looked out over the congregation as though they weren't there, and she patted her foot, impatiently, to speed up the slow hymns. Her foot was the only one that moved in the row of shoes that showed under the short brown curtain that hung in front of the choir.

Silky had followed her into church one time; she went right up into the choir, and Miss Emma held her on her lap until the service was over. When it came time to stand and sing the offertory, Miss Emma stayed in her seat and patted her foot a little faster than the organ and sang with Silky on her lap.

Miss Emma had loved Silky better than anyone or anything. She brushed her and fussed over her and never let her run with the other dogs in the neighborhood. Last spring when it was discovered that Silky was going to have puppies, Mary thought Miss Emma might go crazy over it, she was so upset.

"I just don't know how this happened." Her mouth would clop, over and over, and tears would come in her eyes, and her little face would twitch. Then she quit mentioning it, and nobody else seemed to think much about it except Mary, who was excited and wanted one of the puppies.

One day she went over to Miss Emma's. She walked along the driveway on the narrow side of the yard, under the camphor trees that were planted too close to the house and had to lean out over the graveled paths. At the back porch steps she called through the screened door. "Miss Emma." There was no answer, so she opened the door and started in. Silky lay on her side on the rag rug that Miss Emma used to wipe her shoes when she came in from the yard. Mary knew at once that Silky was dead. There was something brown on her back legs, and her sides were flat and empty looking.

Mary backed down the wood steps. She heard a faint chipping sound down near the cedar. She ran down and found Miss Emma under the tree trying to spade the hard ground.

"What happened? I saw her. What happened?"

"She's dead."

"I know. But what happened? What happened to the puppies?"

"They're dead."

"Oh." Mary pressed her fists to her cheeks.

"Can't I go get someone to come help you? Can't I do something? Where are the puppies?" Mary held a drooping cedar bough away from her face.

Miss Emma's face glistened with sweat. She was making little headway. Her small mouth hung open, and she pressed her foot on the shovel.

Mary turned and pushed through the high privet hedge. Jim was watering his flower beds. His shears lay on the porch.

"Jim! Come help Miss Emma dig a grave for Silky. She's dead from childbirth."

"Gawd. Limme git a box." He turned the water off at the nozzle, and the hose writhed in the grass like a snake that refused to die. Mary turned the water off at the hydrant, and the hose lay down and began to relax.

Jim looked around for a moment, then picked up a large pasteboard Grande Dame coffee box with a label on the top.

"What do you want?" asked Miss Emma. "I can do this."

"No'm," said Jim. "You gimme that shovel, now." And he began to dig. He was a powerful man and soon had a deep hole dug. He fitted the box into it, then took it out. "Now that'll jist about do it," he said. "Where the dog at, Miz Emma?"

Miss Emma said, "Show him, Mary. Wrap her in that rag rug."

Mary and Jim soon returned. The box was closed, but Miss Emma didn't even look at it. She just sat on the cold stone bench. The Grande Dame lady on top of the box looked straight ahead, her wavy hair parted in the middle and her little pink mouth prim. She had a peaceful eye. Jim threw the first spade of dirt into her blank, pretty face. Miss Emma rose. "Thank you both." The cedar raked her hair. Mary heard the back porch door slam.

Jim beat the back of the spade down hard on Silky's grave, and then he stamped the earth heavily with his feet. Mary thought of the picture of the Grande Dame coffee lady staring out forever, with her peaceful eye.

"Ain't nothing but a dog, Miss Mary."

"I know it. Thanks a lot, Jim." And they left.

Later Mary found Miss Emma on her front porch. Mary leaned against the banister, feeling sorry for her.

"What happened to the puppies? How many were there?" She had to know.

"There were six," said Miss Emma. "They are all dead. They had slick short hair — black and white — terrible-looking mongrels just like that beast that belongs to those nigras over there." She indicated the other end of the block by cutting her eyes to her left.

"What did you do with them?"

"I buried them behind the shed after you and the nigra left. The ground is softer back there. They were all born dead."

"Oh . . ."

"I'll go in now. You be careful crossing the street. Look both ways." Miss Emma left Mary, and Mary swung around the post and stepped off the front porch.

She found the fresh mound of earth just beyond the black pot where Sadie did Miss Emma's wash. On the bench under the shed was a galvanized tub half-filled with water. Mary put her hand on the clothesline and leaned forward. A white puppy with black spots floated there. Hair floated around it.

Mary heard her own breath sucked in. The spade leaned against the tub. She was about to reach for it when she heard a sound — a squeak. She froze. The squeak became a chorus. *No! Oh, no, no, no.* Dim baby cries came from the mound. She felt ill, as though she might faint or vomit. She dropped the spade, fell on her knees, and began clawing the damp earth. But she had barely felt the dirt under her nails when Miss Emma's voice rasped, "What do you think you are doing?"

"Please, Miss Emma! They aren't dead! I *hear* the puppies. Maybe we can save them." She lifted her hands from the dirt.

Miss Emma grasped Mary's arms roughly. "Go home immediately, young lady! This is none of your business."

In her own room Mary took a pillow and hid under her bed. She shut her eyes, beat her ears with her palms, felt buried alive under the dark, wet earth. She wrapped the soft pillow around her head and moaned.

It was almost dark when her mother waked her.

"Mary! What are you doing sleeping under the bed? A big girl nearly twelve years old! Come out from under there. Supper's almost ready."

Mary opened her eyes. Mama had turned on the lamp, and she could see dust thick on the baseboard near her face. She felt the same dust lining her nostrils. She clutched her pillow, and crawled out and went to the front porch to look at Miss Emma's house. It had been no dream. And she was going to hear that terrible sound forever. If she couldn't dig them up, why hadn't she . . . but there was nothing she could do. Maybe . . .

She crossed the street. When she stepped behind Miss Emma's shed, she saw in the half-light that the galvanized tub had been emptied and hung on the wall, the molded rings in its bottom barely visible. She listened, one ear turned to the mound. She turned her head enough to know that Miss Emma was close behind her, and though she did not look at her, she knew what that face looked like.

"You forgot to bury one, and the others weren't dead."

"They are now. And they are all buried."

"How — why did you do it?"

"I thought they were dead. I held them under a long time — each one — till they quit squirming and were perfectly still and limp. I thought they were dead."

As she turned to look at Miss Emma, she saw the pale hymn singer patting her foot impatiently in the church choir — Get on with it! Die! I haven't got all day.

"You had done this before you buried Silky."

"This is what I planned to do all along. You forget, Mary, that these were my puppies to do what I please with. They were just mongrel puppies. They might have been cute for a while, but they'd have grown to be ugly dogs — mockeries of my poor Silky. Don't meddle, Mary, or I'll speak to your mother."

Mary knew she would speak to no one. She went home and sat down at the supper table. She slid her knees under the white cloth and began to push food around on her plate, but she couldn't eat.

As the months passed, she heard remarks about Miss Emma. "Emma was always peculiar. But here lately she seems hardly interested in anything." "Emma used to play bridge regularly, but she never picks up a card now." "Emma's just *quit* the Missionary Society." Mary found it easy to avoid Miss Emma, and she learned to avoid pondering the things people were saying. *I don't care about Miss Emma one way or the other.* And in her bed at night when she thought of the little cries, she would turn on her lamp and read until she fell asleep. School started. She had for her teacher the Spanish queen who moved about in a pulsing mist of Appleblossom perfume, and for the first time in her life she felt that she might be the favorite pupil in class — a secret too dizzying to dare breathe to a soul. She was less troubled . . .

Miss Emma's apartment was on the right side overlooking the croquet lawn. Miss Scott and Billy lived on the left. She found, to her surprise, that Miss Scott's door was locked, so she tried another farther down the hall. It was locked. Like it or not, she would have to ask Miss Emma to let her in.

She knocked at her door and got no answer. She rattled the white china knob and found the door bolted. Then she went into Miss Emma's kitchen from the back porch and called, "Miss Emma," into her bedroom. The room was neat, the bed smoothly made, but there was no Miss Emma. Mary went no farther than the bedroom door;

she returned to the kitchen and took Miss Emma's keys off the hook over the gas stove. She quickly found the one to open Miss Scott's apartment. The grade book lay on the bed. She locked up, replaced the keys, and hurried out of the house. This was her lucky day. She walked briskly back to school, swinging the thin blue grade book by her side.

Coming home that afternoon, she noticed two cars in Miss Emma's driveway; also her father's car was home, parked in front of Mrs. Judge Griffith's and Mrs. Doctor Hough's cars. She went in the side door to avoid the living room, but her mother heard her and met her in her room. Something was wrong.

"Mary, honey, something very unfortunate has happened. It's Miss Emma." Mary tilted her head upward and her eyebrows lifted slightly, questioning. Mama's face had never looked quite like this before. There were fine little lines kind of stretched under her eyes, and there was a little shiver in her voice when she said, "She's dead, Mary."

Mary put her books on her desk. The big geography book fell to the floor and opened to a brown and green relief map of South America. Miss Emma was dead. She tried to feel something. *What do I feel? Nothing.*

"What—when did she die? What happened to her?"

"Well, Miss Phaedra walked over there about eleven-thirty this morning, just to look in on her. She found her—dead."

"Found her? Dead at eleven-thirty? Where was she? What happened to her? Did she have a heart attack?"

"No, Mary. She found her lying on the floor beside her bed. She— Darling, she took her own life. Shot herself—Dr. Hough figures she did it about nine this morning."

Nine. Eleven-thirty. "What side of the bed was she on?"

"Why—she was on the side nearest her sitting room. You know— not on the kitchen side, the other side. What makes you ask that?"

"I just wondered—wondered where she—her body was."

"This is such a terrible thing to have to tell a little girl about her friend. I know it's shocking, darling—something awful you've never had to even hear about—you and Miss Emma—friends since you were a baby . . . poor darling . . ." *Poor Mama.*

She leaned her cheek against her mother's arm, and her mother hugged her close. *Poor Mama.* "Poor darling."

"I'm sorry, Mama—I mean it really is terrible, isn't it? But don't worry—about me, I mean."

Her mother left her abruptly because she heard the two ladies— Mrs. Hough and Mrs. Griffith—leaving.

Mary put on her blue slacks, sneakers, and one of her brother's shirts. Later she looked into her mother's room. "Mama, there are only about six blooms in that nasturtium bed under your window. May I pull them up before frost gets them?"

Her mother looked surprised for only a moment. "I wish you would. That's very sweet, Mary." Mary was careful not to slam the screened door.

She dropped to her knees at the bed of summer annuals and began to pull up the spent plants.

"You never can tell about children." Her mother's voice. "Some little girls would have had hysterics." The voice drifted softly from the window. "Of course I didn't go into the bloody details. My Lord! Poor Phaedra, coming on that gruesome . . ." The rich dark soil was cold. It made black arcs under her nails. She crumbled handfuls and sifted it between her fingers, letting it fill holes and depressions.

". . . why? God knows." Her father's voice. "Don't let it prey on your mind, Katherine. I'll have to help with the arrangements. Phaedra can't do it all."

"I know. I know. She took Emma's good beige silk down to the funeral parlor. And she's talked with the brother in New Mexico. He'll be in tomorrow morning on Number 4. He agreed on the phone that Emma of all people should be buried from her church . . ."

"Well, I told Phaedra I'd go out to the cemetery and see that the Lamar lot is trimmed up. I'll take Jim out there . . ."

A katydid struck its one-note song—not a song either, just a note with never a hurry or pause for breath. Katydids must not breathe.

The brittle nasturtiums had shallow roots, and they came up as though they'd never had a grip on the earth. An agile, sherry-colored worm writhed frantically in the loose soil, then disappeared underground. She gathered the plants and broke off the bouquet of remaining blossoms—fragile gold and yellow petals. She added round green leaves with fine white throbless veins. Unfolding her body a little stiffly, she knocked moist dirt from the knees of her slacks.

In the kitchen she stood on a chair to reach a glass — the only one left of her grandmother's heavy old goblets with thistles on the sides, and she took it to the sink and filled it with water. Then she sank the pale, translucent stems into the water and walked to her mother's room. She set the flowers on the desk by the window — on an envelope, so the glass wouldn't make a ring. She rubbed her hands back and forth on the hard smooth surface of the desk that warmed with the friction.

Looking out the window, she saw that Miss Emma's porch was shady and beginning to go lilac the way it sometimes did as the sun sank in the evening. The swing was empty, and the fern baskets hung motionless over the banisters. The big oak tree laid a transparency of itself across the street and over half of Mary's yard. The croquet lawn was smooth and wicketless. She knew the wickets were stored neatly on the back porch with the mallets and balls, their colored bands faded from years of use. The old house smelled of turkey carpets and mothballs. Silky lay beneath the dark cedar with the Grande Dame coffee lady whose face was so peaceful and unworried.

The nasturtiums glowed alive like sunshine in the old goblet on the desk, and Mary felt the hotness of tears in her eyes.

The Man Who Gave Brother Double Pneumonia

I read something in Sunday's paper about a Mississippi girl getting married, a Barbara Dickey Becker, and right then I thought of Mama. I couldn't ever see the name Becker without remembering Mr. Dickey and Mama and Brother and all the rest.

Not long before Mama died somebody asked her, "You remember Mr. Dickey Becker . . . ?" And she interrupted, "Remember him? I reckon I do remember him. He's the one who gave Brother double pneumonia." By that time Daddy was no longer there to stand up for Mr. Dickey, as he had for years, with, "Now, Ellen, you know Dickey wasn't responsible for that. Nobody was to blame." And I always felt like the *nobody* included me.

Mr. Dickey Becker was a barber — one of two in Sweet Bay. Mr. Dickey's was the one with the barber pole that actually turned, its red and white stripes coiling endlessly in its glass cylinder. He didn't even turn it off Sundays. We would drive down Main Street after church, and the only thing moving on the whole street would be Mr. Dickey Becker's barber pole. Mr. Dud Lewis's across the street between the post office and Willey's Feed and Seed had a barber pole, but it was just a painted column of wood, and the paint was flaking off. He didn't ever paint it that I can remember, but he was called a good barber.

During the year when Brother and I were seven Daddy asked Mama to start taking us to Mr. Dickey for our haircuts. Brother had been going to Mr. Lewis, and Mama usually took me with her to Miss Ella B. Jones's Beauty Shoppe. Mama didn't want to take us to Mr. Dickey's, but we were deep in the Depression, and Mr. Dickey owed Daddy some money and couldn't pay it right then. He asked Daddy to trade it out in haircuts for himself and us two. Daddy and Mama argued, but she finally gave in. I pouted and fussed about going to a man's barber shop, where scarcely another female ever showed her face except for mothers who brought their little boys in. Mama came in with us the first time and gave Mr. Dickey instructions. After that she would drop us off and go on to the library or the grocery store or somewhere until time to pick us up. We always had to wait, and if Mama pulled up to the curb out front and saw that we were not through, she would either sit there and read or drive on off for one more errand.

Mr. Dickey's shop was long and narrow like most barber shops. He had three chairs, with a big white porcelain lavatory behind each chair. Several long benches for waiting customers sat along the opposite wall. Mirrors lined both walls, and large milk glass lighting fixtures hung down the center, two with ceiling fans attached. There were lots of jars and bottles behind Mr. Dickey and a stack of white towels, and under the lavatory a white wicker hamper where he threw wet towels.

Brother and I had haircuts every three weeks or so. At twenty-five cents a cut, Mama said, Mr. Dickey would never on this earth retire his debt in his lifetime. We went there only through the summer and halfway through the winter of 1933 — until Brother got double pneumonia.

One afternoon in early January, Mama bundled us up to go down to Mr. Dickey's — with me protesting. Daddy was at home.

"Why don't you like Mr. Dickey?" Daddy finally asked me.

"He teases me."

"How does he tease you, Sister?"

"He calls me a boy. He says I don't have long curls like other girls. He says my bangs and my short bob are for boys, and I hate him."

"No, now, you don't hate anybody. Mr. Dickey's not a bad fellow. He and I are good friends from way back."

"I don't care. I do hate him."

"Ah, Sister." Then Daddy laughed. "I'll tell you what you do. If he teases you today, tell him he's a ring-tailed tooter."

"Thad!" Mama whirled around.

"Tell him that. You tell him your daddy says he's a ring-tailed tooter."

"No," I said. "I'm not telling him anything. What is a ring-tailed tooter?"

"Doesn't matter what it is. Just call him that. You can tell him that he's the only barber you ever heard of who barbers all week, bootlegs on Saturday night, and preaches on Sunday."

"Thaddeus!"

"Does he do all that?" I asked.

"Sure he does. You don't think he supports that big family of his cutting hair for two bits a head, do you?"

"Thad, I want this stopped this minute. You cannot talk to a seven-year-old child like that. It's one thing for you and him to keep up this foolishness between the two of you, but I will not have Sister going down there speaking disrespectfully to Mr. Dickey. I don't care what he does with his weekends."

I was trying to count up how many children Mr. Dickey had to feed and clothe on haircutting. "Well," I said, "he sells bottles of hair tonic and other stuff."

"Now stop right there, Sister. There'll be no impudence to Mr. Becker or to anyone else," said Mama. "But I do want you to remind him not to put a drop of anything on Brother's hair. Not one drop. I've told him time and again not to use hair tonic on Brother, but he forgets, I reckon, and does it anyway. Every time. But this is pneumonia weather, and I don't want Brother coming out of there with a wet head. Will you remember to tell him?" She was pulling Brother's leather helmet over his blond softly curling hair and snapping the tabs under his chin.

"Yes'm, I'll tell him. But I don't want to go in there." I had on brown cotton stockings that fastened to my short union suit — a getup nobody else's mother made them wear no matter how cold it got. I decided I was already so tacky that having my hair cut in a man's barber shop couldn't add much to my misery. Brother and I got into Mama's car arguing over who would ride in the front seat with her, and of course Brother won. He always did. He was frail, and Mama had to let him have his own way because she was afraid he would have one of his tantrums and throw up.

I got onto the backseat and slipped down so that my neck bent up against the back and so my feet could push hard against the back of Brother's seat. "Mama, tell her to stop," he whined.

"Mercy sakes, Sister, sit up like a lady. The idea."

I sat up and watched the houses go by, most of them white, with the rocking chairs turned over against the wall on the cold front porches. It was five blocks to the barber shop, and Mama stopped at each corner to look every which way, even when she had the right-of-way. She was like that. Daddy would say, "Ellen, caution is your middle name." And she would say, "Well, mark my word, Thaddeus, I'd rather be a live monkey than a dead heroine." She had picked that up from Daddy, only he said *hero*.

There were hardly any other cars on the streets that day. There weren't all that many cars in Sweet Bay. There weren't all that many people. And on cold days they mostly stayed in around the fire. You won't find long winters in south Mississippi, but there are always a few freezing days.

Mama wore a hat every time she went anywhere, and that day she had on a little hat made of curly fur, shaped like a soufflé dish, with a coat collar to match. She wore black kid gloves that had little rows of stitching on the backs, and the way she gripped the steering wheel made the gloves shine and look as tight as her skin.

She pulled up along the curb in front of Mr. Dickey's. *Becker's Barber Shop* was painted in big red letters on the window, arched like a rainbow and with white shadings painted along the right side of each red letter. The sign kept you from seeing everything in the shop, but I could see Mr. Dickey flipping his razor back and forth on the leather strop that hung off the back of his chair. He had the first chair, near the window, and I saw him looking out at us. He had a big fat customer in his chair.

Mama made Brother crawl over her so he wouldn't have to get out in the street and maybe get run over. There was hardly a car moving but, as I said, she never took any chances. He just stepped all over her and she said, "Well, for heaven's sake, Brother. I think you could be a little more careful. Now, trot straight in there and stay till I come back for you."

I got out of the back, sulking, as she said, "Sister, remember I'm depending on you. Don't you dare let Mr. Dickey put hair tonic on Brother's head. As sure as I'm sitting here that child will come out in this pneumonia weather and catch his death."

"I'll tell him," I said, slamming the door so hard that I spun myself all the way around. I caught my scarf in the door, and Mama was about to drive away with it pulling right off my neck till I called, "Mama, wait!" She shoved her foot down quickly and stopped. She really hadn't moved two feet, but she rolled her window down while I opened the back door and got my scarf loose.

"I declare to my soul, Sister, I don't know what I'm going to do with you! Now that was careless. If I hadn't been paying attention to what I was doing, no telling what might have happened to you. Now go on in there while I sit here and see you in. March!" I went into the barber shop.

"Hurry up, Ellen. Hurry that door closed. You'll blow us out of here," said Mr. Dickey. I shut his old door carefully. I say old because it was *old,* a big old tall door with glass and carving and a funny big brass handle shaped like a swan. I rattled it good when I shut it.

"Just have a seat there by Brother and I'll get to you-all directly, Sister." Mr. Dickey would call me *Sister* one minute and *Ellen* the next.

I took off my cap, coat, gloves, scarf, and balled them up on the bench beside me.

"You better take off your helmet," I said to Brother. "And your jacket, too. If you sit in here by the stove in them, they won't feel as warm when you go back out in the cold." I'm twenty-five minutes older than he is, and I was taller than he was then, and Mama held me accountable for whatever happened to either one of us. He had the Bible stories, just turning the pages. I knew he was looking for the colored pictures. He couldn't read except in his reader and only about the front half of that.

"You better," I said.

"I am not. You can't tell me what to do. You're not my boss."

Mr. Dickey looked over at us and said, "Which one of you-all

is the boy and which one is the girl? I never can tell." He looked
at me and squinted his eyes like he couldn't see the difference perfectly well and said, "Oh, now I see, you're the girl — Miss Ellen
Warner. Little Miss Warner. Ain't that right?"

I guess I looked at him kind of dumb. I thought he sounded silly.
But since I had his attention I blurted, "Mr. Dickey, don't put hair
tonic on Brother's head. Mama said to tell you. She said don't dare
do it or he'll catch his death."

"Aw. Did your mama say that, Brother? You got that real leather
helmet, fleece lined, and she's ascairt of a little tonic wetting your
head?"

"You better do what my mama said," I said louder. "She *told* me
to tell you."

Brother dropped the book and slid way down to the other end
of his bench and kind of fell over to one side like an idiot and didn't
say a word. He just looked at Mr. Dickey and down at the other
barbers. Brother was plenty smart, but a lot of the time he liked
to act like he didn't have a brain in his head. He wasn't any distance
from that stove, which was red hot, and he still had on his helmet
and jacket. Just because I told him to take them off. I just hushed
up about it. Let him sweat.

I could see us in the mirror behind Mr. Dickey. And I could see
what was in our mirror in Mr. Dickey's mirror, and it went on like
that, everything just reflecting itself over and over again across the
narrow shop. I figured the only way to stop that was to wait till it
was night and turn off the lights to make it pitch black.

Finally Brother took his helmet off, and his jacket, and let them
fall on the floor. Cubby came along with his broom and his dust-
pan with the long handle, sweeping up hair around the chairs, and
he picked up Brother's things and hung them on the pegs by the door.

"Here, let me hang yo's up, too, Miss Sister," he said. I thanked
him, aware of how much better my manners were than Brother's.
That's what came of being a girl, I thought. Boys just naturally didn't
have any manners.

"So you are a little girl, after all," Mr. Dickey started up again.
He talked that way, smiling at me like he was doing me a favor to
tell the whole room what everybody in town knew. I didn't look up.

I picked up the Bible stories and opened them to a drawing of a man in a long gown looking out over the ocean. A fisher of men, it said. But I was listening to Mr. Dickey, who was talking to me at the same time he was talking to his customer.

It was Old Man Duff Willey. I wouldn't have called him Old Man Willey out loud, of course, but that's what I'd heard him called. I hadn't recognized him at first because Mr. Dickey had his face covered with a hot towel, and his body, which was stretched out like he was in bed, was almost covered by the sheet Mr. Dickey put over you for a haircut. Old Man Willey had a huge stomach and black hightops. His ankles were crossed on the silver metal prop that grown people could rest their feet on. His shoes were shiny, and I figured Cubby had been there popping his shoeshine rag on them before we came in.

When Mr. Dickey took off the towel Old Man Willey came up like a whale, and Mr. Dickey pulled off the sheet and raised the back of the chair and lowered the footrest — all at one time. Then he turned and popped the sheet like a whip. Pow! Brother sat up. He liked a big racket. He started laughing like he was crazy, and Mr. Dickey winked at him and began laughing big like it was funny, like it was something only he and Brother knew about. That's the kind of thing I didn't like about going to a man's barber shop.

Old Man Willey's face was red as a beet. He had red, white, and blue eyes that sat in puffy bags. His eyebrows were white and bushy, and his hair was just a white circle around his bald head. His head was as red as his face. He reached down in his pocket and got some change to pay Mr. Dickey and then got his coat off the wall peg. Old Man Willey smiled big and walked over, all bundled up, and snapped his big pink fingers back of Brother's ear, like a magician.

"Well, will you looka there, boy. Look what I found ahint your ear." And he gave Brother a whole dime. Then he patted Brother on the head and said, "Pretty little fellow. Look at them eyelashes. You sure oughta been a girl, son." Then he walked on past me without so much as a kiss my foot and rattled the old door closed behind him.

Brother closed his fist around the dime. I knew from the way he did it I would never see a penny of it. Not that it mattered. I had a nickel at home under Mama's dresser scarf, and Daddy would always give me another if I asked him, even with the Depression on him.

Mr. Dickey shook his sheet again, only this time he didn't pop it. "All righty," he said, looking first at Brother, then at me, "who's next?" Brother just sat there clutching his dime. "Ladies first?" Mr. Dickey bowed toward me.

Of course that waked Brother up. "No, I want to be first," he said, and jumped off the bench. Mr. Dickey was getting his children's board that he kept leaning against the wall under the lavatory. Brother climbed up to the footrest and onto the black leather seat, standing there tall as anything while Mr. Dickey laid the board across the arms. "All righty, little feller, just set it down right there."

When Brother sat, Mr. Dickey flipped the big sheet over him and fastened it behind his neck with a safety pin. The sheet hung over Brother and the whole chair like a white tent, and his head looked like a little round babydoll with blonde curls and big blue eyes. Mama cried the first time Brother's curls were cut. Daddy cut them off himself because he was afraid people would think Brother was a girl. That wasn't a bad idea because Brother was pretty, I had to admit. I didn't get nearly so much chin-chuckling and cheek-pinching as he did. Brother could smile like an angel. And he was right sweet on occasion.

Mr. Dickey began snipping, and the soft pale hair fell over the sheet and onto the floor. Some fell over Brother's face, and when he tried to blow it off his own face he made a loud noise. He and I began to giggle and we couldn't stop. Finally Mr. Dickey just left the comb sticking in Brother's hair and held the scissors down by his side. "Now you younguns got to stop this foolishness. I can't cut hair if you don't behave yourselves. You don't want me to cut your ear off, do you, Brother? You wanta see red blood running down all over that white sheet?"

Brother got still. But I kept on giggling.

"What's that boy giggling about over there, Brother? That boy in that dress with them brown stockings? Ain't that a boy just giggling to beat the band over there on my bench?"

Brother said, "Yeah," just the way Mama told us not to say it to grown folks. But I knew he wasn't thinking about a thing in this world but getting out of that chair and down to Mr. Claude Corbett's drugstore, just as fast as his legs would carry him, to get a double-dip with his dime. I could just see it, chocolate in one side and vanilla in the other. And not one lick for me. He would make himself sick and throw up all over himself before he would give me a lick. And who would get blamed for his ruining his supper? He didn't hear a word Mr. Dickey was saying.

"You know what you are?"

At first Mr. Dickey thought I was talking to Brother. Then he caught on to me talking to him. He smiled friendly and said, "What am I, little Miss?" I think he was expecting me to say *he* was a girl.

"You are—you are a ring-tailed tooter."

Well, I wish you could have seen him. He just stood there for a minute and I knew I had, as Daddy would say, fired a big gun. I didn't know what I was talking about, and in fact I do not to this day.

"Well, now, where'd you pick up such talk? Shame on you! Shame on you!" Mr. Dickey didn't like it. I could tell. I began to figure I had been too sassy, and I started wondering just how bad a ring-tailed tooter was. I tried to smile pretty big and looked right at Mr. Dickey Becker. Brother wasn't even listening; I knew where his mind was. Then Mr. Dickey began to laugh again.

"But that's right. You're a boy, ain't you? And that's boy talk." He laughed.

"I am not a boy."

"Sure you are. Look at that straight hair. How come you don't have them big eyes and long eyelashes like a girl ought to? Wouldn't you say that was a boy, Brother?"

His teasing fired me up again. I took a deep breath and said, "And you are a barber today. But Saturday you will be a bootlegger selling whiskey to the ignoramuses. And Sunday you will preach hell and thunderation to the multitude in that Baptist church out by Hickson's cotton gin." I tucked my chin and looked sideways to the back of the shop. Everybody began laughing.

Mr. Dickey had been putting powder on Brother's neck and dusting it off like clouds of smoke with his soft round brush. He held still a little bit. Then he laughed and shook his head. "I'll be dawged.

If that ain't Thad Warner talking, I'm a monkey's uncle. Your daddy put you up to that, young lady."

"Lady?" yelled Brother, like somebody who suddenly had come to his senses. "How can she be a young lady if she's a boy?" See? That's what I mean about him acting like he had good sense sometimes. But then he began to laugh like crazy. He did that every now and then, just began laughing real loud, hollering really. His best friend, Junior Henderson, did the same thing, so I figured it wasn't unnatural.

Everybody was so jolly over my big joke that I felt better, until all of a sudden I realized Mr. Dickey had that narrow-necked bottle upside down over Brother's head, shaking it like he was trying to get catsup out. Before I knew it Brother's head was sopping wet.

"Mr. Dickey Becker! Mr. Dickey Becker! You've put hair tonic on my brother's head."

"Oh, law me," he said, like he really had not meant to do something wrong. Well, I had told him. He grabbed a huck towel and began rubbing Brother's hair. He rubbed it and rubbed it. When he took the towel off, Brother looked like a doll that had fallen in the washtub. His hair stuck out every which way, and it was still wet.

"Aw, it's almost dry, Sister," said Mr. Dickey. He combed it forward like bangs over Brother's forehead. Then he parted it straight as an arrow on one side and combed the sides down straight. He combed the top to one side and whipped a neat cowlick back over Brother's forehead. "Now, just looka there. That's a pretty child." He was talking to the mirror over my head. "And by the time Mrs. Warner drives up out there, that hair will be as dry as a bone." He took the sheet off and popped it.

In a wink Brother slid down off the board, onto the seat, down to the footrest, and off onto the floor. He made a beeline for the door. I couldn't even scream, "Brother, come back here!" before he was out in that pneumonia weather with his wet head, flying down the street to the drugstore for a double-dip. I just knew Mama would drive up right then. But she didn't.

I grabbed my things and Brother's helmet and jacket and tore out after him. Mr. Claude Corbett already had his scoop down in the chocolate when I ran in through the back door where children weren't even allowed. Brother was up on the stool, leaning on his elbows way over the marble counter so he could see down into the ice cream cans.

"Brother, what'd you do that for? Are you just plain crazy? Mama's going to die, just plain die. Put on your jacket and helmet this minute before she comes and sees you." He got his cone and laid Old Man Willey's dime on the counter. Then he got down and let me put the jacket and helmet on him. He never missed a lick on his cone, just switched it from one hand to the other while he put his arms into the sleeves. Ice cream was all over his face by the time I dragged him back up to the barber shop.

We had no more than gotten inside when there was Mama's car.

"Here, now, Sister," said Mr. Dickey. "What about your haircut?"

"I'll have to come back," I said to the ring-tailed tooter, who was just sitting there in his own barber chair perfectly unconcerned over what had happened. I didn't want him to have a chance to speak to Mama again and tell her I'd been impudent.

Mama hadn't turned the engine off; because of the cold she might have had trouble starting up again. She was just sitting there sort of daydreaming, looking straight ahead. She didn't notice the ice cream on Brother's chin and cheeks, or that my hair wasn't trimmed under my cap. She had library books all over the front seat, so Brother had to get on the backseat with me. I accidentally stepped on his foot, and he hit me on my arm and made it hurt. "Mama," he hollered, "she made me drop my ice cream." He picked up all he could off the seat and tried to stuff it back in the cone.

"Ice cream? Where on earth did you get ice cream? Don't you know it will give you the sorest kind of throat to eat ice cream in weather like this? What are we coming to when a druggist, a graduate pharmacist from the University of Mississippi, will sell ice cream to children in 40-degree weather and snow threatened all over Mississippi tonight? My soul and body!"

By the time she had said all that, we were under the porte cochere. Brother crawled all over me getting out of the car, so he could beat me up the steps.

Mama and I followed him, with her saying, "Lord have mercy, Sister, what have you let him get into?"

Once inside the house she seemed to notice everything at once — chocolate and vanilla ice cream on Brother's face, hands, and clothes, my hair not cut, Brother's helmet hanging crooked, not snapped. Then she looked thunderstruck, and she pulled off the helmet like she feared the worst.

"Sister! What did I tell you? Would you look? For pity's sake, his nose is already running." It was, too. She pulled off his coat. "Oleander!" I almost said *Mama hollered,* but of course Mama didn't holler, not like Brother and I hollered. But she kind of shrieked this time. Oleander came running.

"Draw us a hot tub of water, Oleander. Quickly!"

"What done happen to our boy, Miss Ellen?"

"That old . . . Mr. Dickey Becker wet his head with hair tonic and sent him out in the cold."

"Well, you ain't about to put him in no water after such exposin', are you?"

"Of course not. I want to keep him in there in the steam so he won't stop up. Get a blanket and the Vicks and bring them in there. Then don't let a soul dare open that door." As she led Brother into the bathroom he began to sneeze. They stayed in there a long time, Mama's and Oleander's voices rising and falling, Brother's voice breaking over theirs, cranky and mad.

Brother got pneumonia. It took him two days to really get it, but he got sick that night after the haircut and he got sicker all the next day, when Mama called Dr. Butler. He came right then, like he always did, and his little black coupé was in our driveway twice a day for about a week. Mama hardly ever left Brother. Daddy tiptoed in and out. They got Miss Ruby Burris, the trained nurse, to come, and she stayed day and night taking Brother's temperature and helping to hold the mustard poultices up to the fireplace so they could lay them hot on Brother's chest.

Mama closed the piano and turned off the radio. She didn't even come to the table. She talked about "sending for the girls," our two sisters who were away at school. Daddy's sister, who didn't even like Mama, came from down the street with a tureen of gumbo "for the family." Mama happened to be in the hall, and she kissed Aunt

Minnie and said kindly, "Thank you, Minnie." Now I was sure
Brother was going to die.

"Is it really *double* pneumonia, Ellen?"

"Yes, Minnie. Both lungs."

I spent a lot of time sitting on the footstool in the living room.
Nobody accused me of anything, but I felt pretty sure that if Brother
didn't get well they would think it was my fault. And it would be
true. I could have stood at the door and stopped him. I had known
he was going to head out for that ice cream. The minute Old Man
Willey gave him the dime, I knew it. Why hadn't I stopped him?
Why hadn't I watched Mr. Dickey when he picked up the bottle?

Then on about the seventh day Dr. Butler came out of Mama and
Daddy's room, which was the sickroom, and he said to Daddy, "Well,
Thad, he's passed the crisis." And Daddy put his arm across Doctor's
shoulders and said, "Thank God, Henry. Thank God." Doctor came
in the living room, stretching and sort of grunting like he was relieved and thinking about some rest now. He saw me sitting in
Mama's chair by the fire.

"Sister, you're looking a little peaked yourself. Are you feeling
well?"

"Yes, sir."

"Well, don't look so unhappy. Your brother is going to be all right.
You ought to cheer up. You're sure you aren't feeling poorly? Stick
out your tongue." He came over and held my wrist and peered down
at me through his bifocals. "No, you're fine. Cool as a cucumber."

"I'm the one that made him sick."

"You're what?"

"I let him out in the cold with his head wet after he got his hair cut."

"Sister!" He dropped into Daddy's chair and pulled me against
his knee, and I cried and cried and told him the whole thing.

"Sister Warner, your brother's pneumonia had nothing to do with
Mr. Dickey's hair tonic. I want you to promise me you'll forget such
nonsense." He took out a clean handkerchief and patted my eyes,
then he shook the folds out and put it under my nose. "Here, now,
blow!" Then he stood up and stuffed his handkerchief in his coat
pocket. He wrinkled his nose to push his glasses up higher. He did
that all the time. It was funny. He would make that quick funny

little face, and it would push his glasses up, but then they would slip right down again on his thin straight nose. I wanted to hug his neck, but I didn't.

In a few days I was allowed to go in and play on the bed with Brother. He had so many new toys there was hardly any room. Oleander made him a big vanilla milkshake every day to build him up, and she made me one, too, even though I didn't need any building up. Brother liked the milkshake and drank every drop till I told him it had a raw egg in it. Then he wouldn't touch it. He threw a fit if anybody even brought it in the room. Mama was outdone with me for telling him about the raw egg, but she didn't make much of it.

And one day she just up and told me it wasn't my fault at all that Brother got pneumonia. Daddy said good gracious no. Never in a million years. He said it was nobody's fault. But Mama believed to her dying day that Mr. Dickey Becker gave Brother double pneumonia. We never had to go back to his barber shop. Brother started going over to Lewis's again. He told me Mr. Lewis didn't use a nice soft brush to dust the powder off his neck like Mr. Dickey. "He blows it off," said Brother, "and when it gets in your face, he blows right in your face." Brother stretched his mouth down in the corners and held his nose.

Mama began taking me with her again to Miss Ella B.'s Beauty Shoppe, where I had a wonderful time watching ladies get their hair dipped in blueing or get hooked up to the electrical permanent wave machines. Miss Ella B. even talked Mama into letting my hair grow long to plait.

Daddy kept going to Mr. Dickey's for his haircuts and his shoeshines. He said it gave Mr. Dickey a painless way to make a payment on his loan, and besides, Daddy didn't want him to get his feelings hurt about the double pneumonia.

ILLINOIS SHORT FICTION

Crossings by Stephen Minot
A Season for Unnatural Causes by Philip F. O'Connor
Curving Road by John Stewart
Such Waltzing Was Not Easy by Gordon Weaver

Rolling All the Time by James Ballard
Love in the Winter by Daniel Curley
To Byzantium by Andrew Fetler
Small Moments by Nancy Huddleston Packer

One More River by Lester Goldberg
The Tennis Player by Kent Nelson
A Horse of Another Color by Carolyn Osborn
The Pleasures of Manhood by Robley Wilson, Jr.

The New World by Russell Banks
The Actes and Monuments by John William Corrington
Virginia Reels by William Hoffman
Up Where I Used to Live by Max Schott

The Return of Service by Jonathan Baumbach
On the Edge of the Desert by Gladys Swan
Surviving Adverse Seasons by Barry Targan
The Gasoline Wars by Jean Thompson

Desirable Aliens by John Bovey
Naming Things by H. E. Francis
Transports and Disgraces by Robert Henson
The Calling by Mary Gray Hughes

Into the Wind by Robert Henderson
Breaking and Entering by Peter Makuck
The Four Corners of the House by Abraham Rothberg
Ladies Who Knit for a Living by Anthony E. Stockanes